The Snowy Road and Other Stories

The Snowy Road and Other Stories

An Anthology of Korean Fiction

Edited by
Hyun-jae Yee Sallee

Translated by
Hyun-jae Yee Sallee & Dr. Teresa Margadonna Hyun

WHITE PINE PRESS

Publication of this book was made possible, in part, by grants from the
National Endowment for the Arts, the New York State Council on the
Arts, and the Korean Culture and Arts Foundation.

Published by White Pine Press
76 Center Street, Fredonia, New York 14063

First printing, 1993

Printed in the United States of America

Book design by Watershed Design

ISBN 1-877727-19-9

Contents

The Snowy Road and Other Stories

Introduction

Modern Korean fiction may seem to the prospective reader to be something of an acquired taste. The stories in the American press about Korea's economic development, trade issues, reunification talks between north and south, already seem distant enough, and the 1988 Seoul Olympics have been displaced by the recent Winter games, and anticipation of Barcelona. Yet, interestingly, in all these stories Korea is very much part of the world of news: an economic partner, Olympic venue; an important political factor in Asia. No longer, in any event, is Korea the poor foreign country that served as the backdrop to the Army soap opera M.A.S.H., a television program that was more a predecessor to General Hospital than a documentary on Korean cultural life.

Korea's history, even in just the span of this century, has been a hard one. Occupied as a colony by Japan from 1910 until 1945, Korea was liberated when Japan was defeated at the end of the Second World War, and then immediately divided for no good reason into southern and northern zones which became regimes that gave nation-status to the political split between Left and Right. From these muddled origins—foreign interference, the dashed hopes for national autonomy, and the serious structural inequities that had been part of pre-modern Korean society and which the Japanese occupation exacerbated—came the Korean War, which broke out in 1950. Like all civil wars, the Korean War was especially brutal and violent, and made all the more destructive by the participation of the United States and United Nations fighting on the southern side, and the Russian equipment and hundreds of thousands of Chinese soldiers involved with the north. By the time the Korean War had ended, perhaps as many as three million Korean people had died, roughly one-tenth of the total population of the country. Since the 1953 cease-fire, Korea has led a divided national life under a series of military officers turned civilian presidents in the south, and the so-called "Great and Fearless Leader" Kim II Sung in the north. From such a setting, one might well expect only the most harrowing or hopelessly bleak examples of literature to result.

But literature does not merely reflect the conditions of its creation, in Korea any more than in the United States, or anywhere else; and while there are many instances of seemingly direct representation in Korean literature of recent events, or of more general social and political conditions, the works are the creations of a people who have shown remarkable strength in their belief in humanity, and a tenacious ability to discover moments of individual transcendence in the midst of the most devastating calamity or enduring sadness and pain.

Such are the stories gathered here. They do not reveal the earnestly quaint "Koreans" trotted out in the M.A.S.H. episodes, whose odd intrusions added bits of local color to the essentially American hospital story; nor are they the high powered bosses of government and the business cartels who have engineered the South Korean economic success story of the last ten years. For the most part, these stories tell of other people and their lives, ordinary people, farmers, folk who live somewhere other than

Seoul, almost a country unto itself. The stories describe how these people have gone about making a life under difficult circumstances, through years of incredible change. The remarkable thing is how open these stories are to the outside reader. Observe the way they take their shapes as stories, and listen to how they are told. Note how well they work as stories, using the realistic situations of Korean life as the framing pieces for the plot. Ick-Suh Yoo's "Purchased Bridegroom" for example, is not a sociological study of Korean marriage practices, but a Kafka-esque narrative in which the narrator is, in effect, transformed by his business-like marriage into something like an insect. The story works by snaring the narrator in its turns and twists, and drawing the reader along after to find out the answer to the storyteller's most sought-after response: "So, then what happened?"

One can only wonder how the telling of the story will change, as it must, when the two halves of Korea once again are joined.

—David R. McCann
Cornell University

Translator's Preface

This collection deals largely with Korean family life during the Korean War, the post-war era of the '50s, the agrarian problems of the '60s, and the complexity of city life in the '70s and '80s. The upper classes in Korean society are not often seen in this collection. Instead, the stories are written about lower class life and its poverty, sorrow, and pitiful living conditions. It deals with the heartrending conditions of people victimized first by war and then by industrial and technical development in modern Korea: land improvement programs failed due to drastically centralized economic efforts in the cities necessitated by mass migrations of people to urban areas. The collection also gives the reader a sense of the joy and pain of ordinary city people who became "misfits" by their failure to adjust to the ceaselessly fast-changing city lifestyle and were thus pushed to the outside perimeter of the city.

The stories have a similar and undeniably Eastern flavor with neither dramatic incident nor tantalizing episode. Not one story overtly concerns itself with large social issues or political/economic situations, nor do they indulge in social criticism. The spare style and quiet tone of the stories gives readers insight into what is unique about Korean literature, a technique that might be compared to watching a gentle ripple on a pond.

Yean-hee Chung is critically acclaimed in Korea, where she has received numerous literary awards. Her literary works deal primarily with people who are affected by a modern society that has evolved too rapidly for them. "Balloon" portrays the loneliness of an eight-year-old girl who is a war victim. In a strikingly beautiful style, Ms. Chung captures each detail and circumstance of life in the village while revealing the bleakness of the villagers' existence.

"Purchased Bridegroom" by Ick-suh Yoo, a story about a young man who marries the crippled daughter of his employer and is later betrayed by her, conveys Mr. Yoo's belief that one should live within one's own boundaries.

"The Trap" by Bum-shin Park concerns itself with the shamanism that prevails widely in Korea, especially among poorly educated people, and shows the tragedy of war and the deep scars that remain long after the war is over. An aged woman believes that a dog is the reincarnation of her late husband, while her son believes the dog is an evil spirit and determines to detroy it, and this conflict between generations brings a bizarre ending.

Jung-rae Cho's "Echo, Echo" covers the era of turmoil when Korea was under the Japanese rule, the duration of the Korean War, and the early sixties' political, economic, and social disarray and reflects the unrest and conflict of these times.

"The Snowy Road" by Chung-joon Yee describes the timeless and universal love of a mother for her son despite the sharp contrast between a lonely, poverty-stricken woman in the country and a cold-hearted, city-dwelling son.

Wan-suh Park's "Winter Outing" describes the psychological conflict of a middle-aged woman who was a victim of the war. It points out, in its quiet way, how people are still suffering from the war and its aftermath.

BALLOON
(A SAGA OF MYUNG-AE, THE WIFE OF AN ARTIST, AT NINE YEARS OF AGE)

YEAN-HEE CHUNG

A t daybreak, the sound of the waterbirds' flapping wings resounding in the remnants of darkness filled the air. They opened the curtain of the sky, still carrying the last shrouds of darkness in their beaks. As the sky's curtain was drawn aside, the sun, soundly sleeping until now, stretched its arms.

"Waterbirds usher forth the morning. If it were not for them, morning would never come." The little girl, Young-joo, stood by the window that was directly facing the ocean, absorbed in thought. "The bird flying silently must be the one carrying the last cloak of darkness, and the singing bird must be applauding for the quiet one."

"Hey, you! Why does a little girl like you look so pitiful so early in the morning? Why don't you put some rice on this chopped seaweed and season it for us with a drop of sauce, hum? Hurry up!"

Young-joo's two older sisters, each as large as a horse, had to catch the 6:09 train. If they missed the morning train, they also missed school that day. The train station was located at the tip of the island, and at times, the train looked like a seal that had just come on shore. Her two sisters commuted by train to school in the city. The trip took nearly two hours.

Nine past six in the morning was a somewhat dreadful time. Nothing else intimidated her two sisters, but as 6:09 neared, they could not function properly.

One of them had prepared breakfast; a breakfast table, already set, had been placed in the room. However, they were fretfully neglecting breakfast, fearing that they might miss the train. They were making a great fuss, tidying school bags, combing hair, donning school uniforms, and putting on socks as if they were about to turn the whole world inside out with their vigorous efforts. They couldn't possibly enjoy breakfast in peace. Because of this, Young-joo, their baby sister, carelessly cut the dried seaweed. Dispassionately, she seasoned a spoonful of rice with a drop of soy sauce, then wrapped it with seaweed. Her two sisters would take this food with them and eat it for breakfast whenever they could.

"Oh, my word, I tell you, don't you think our baby sister is the best when it comes to serving breakfast for us this way?"

"Oh, yes, she certainly is. She looks ten times older than she really is. She is like an eighty-year-old woman when she helps us with breakfast!" the other sister replied.

The two older sisters snatched the seaweed-wrapped rice and put it into their mouths while completing preparations for school. As soon as the wall clock began to strike six, they rushed out in a flurry, like wounded animals. In the midst of such a hurry, her second oldest sister, Sun-joo, in the eighth grade, never forgot to give daily instructions to her baby sister.

"Young-joo, you have to go to school today, do you understand? When the clock strikes eight times, that's the time for you to leave for school. I'll go to your school and find out whether you were in class or not."

Although Young-joo nodded her head, she knew very well that her sister's remark about going to school to check on her was a lie. Her sister, Sun-joo, was not only pretty but also bright; nevertheless, she frequently made intimidating or spiteful remarks. Young-joo had never seen her sister act on this threat, however. In this household of only three girls, Sun-joo, the second oldest, appeared to be the only one who had any strength of character. She managed to keep the entire household running smoothly, yet Young-joo knew her sister had a soft heart.

The prior spring, their father had passed away and soon after, their mother had started a business. Before the death of their father, they led an adequately comfortable life due to the considerable savings their parents had put aside during the three years of the refugee era before the turmoil of wartime. Losing their father was a crushing experience.

The girls did not know what business their mother was engaged in. She came home only once a week. Sometimes she was gone for ten days. When and if she dropped in, she usually left a large sum of cash to the oldest one, Moon-joo, who spent all the money purchasing socks, undergarments, or snacks for herself. Consequently, she found herself in great trouble, indebted to the general store in the neighborhood.

Housemaids, who without proper supervision could run the housekeeping in any way they desired, soon began to steal from the family and would then disappear. This happened frequently. Moon-joo, only caring about her spending money, took these matters lightly.

Sun-joo was the one who mainly pressed the maid about the stealing problem. Once some money was missing, and the three girls were filled with concern. This anxiety turned into anger, which drove Sun-joo to urge the maid to confess. As night deepened, she summoned the maid, who was about the same age as herself, and began to severely question her.

Despite Sun-joo's harsh interrogation, the maid flatly denied any knowledge of the theft. Angered, Sun-joo made a strange threat.

"Are you really going to deny this? I went to a Buddhist temple to ask about the proper tactics for catching a thief. Do you know what the monk's advice was? If I chant a prayer to catch a thief while I poke a boiled egg with a needle, the thief becomes blind. Do you think I should try that same formula on you at this moment?"

Young-joo had no way of finding out whether or not Sun-joo's challenge had intimidated the maid into confessing her crime. After that incident, another arose, involving their mother's ring. This time it was another maid who went through a similar method of questioning by Sun-joo, who exercised the same strategy, cornering the maid sharply at midnight.

"Have you ever heard the story of using a cat to catch a thief? Let me tell you about it. You see, if someone prays for help in catching a thief while poking the eyes of a cat with a needle, the thief loses his eyesight completely. Would you like me to try the same thing on our cat right now?" Sun-joo spoke in a clear, calm voice, not even blinking her eyes.

That incident faded away, like the previous one, leaving a question mark in Young-joo's heart as to whether her mother's ring had ever been recovered.

Since those two affairs, Young-joo experienced a frequent dream. In it, she saw either hundreds of needles stuck in a shelled, boiled egg or a blue needle stuck in each of a cat's eyes. At times, she saw a tiny bud or bead-like dew forming around the needles which were stuck in the cat's eyes. Young-joo had loved to eat boiled eggs. Now she had become afraid to eat them, even when they were prepared in her favorite style. Furthermore, whenever she saw a cat in real life, Young-joo now warned the cat in a low, urgent tone of voice: "You'd better run away fast. Don't let yourself be caught by my sister, Sun-joo. I'm telling you now, you must hide somewhere before your eyes get poked out with needles. Run along, please!"

More maids were hired, followed by more disgraceful stealing affairs. The maids left as quickly as they came.

Right after her two sisters rushed out, Young-joo studied the room quickly. A nightgown was lying on the floor where it had been casually tossed. There were carelessly thrown hand towels, a messy mirror stand, chopped dried seaweed, and cold, cooked rice, now dried out. Young-joo stood up and approached the window as if she had urgent business there.

The face of the blue sea was swelling. White waterbirds were flying over the sea after delivering darkness somewhere else.

"I don't mind serving my sisters their breakfast every morning. I just hope a housemaid doesn't come to our home again. I don't undertand what makes them steal things that don't belong to them. If they didn't do such things, I know one would stay with us for a long, long time. Besides, my sister, Sun-joo wouldn't need to tell the story about a boiled egg or a needle in a cat's eyes." Young-joo pondered these thoughts.

The white waterbirds seemed to beckon her. Suddenly, Young-joo completely forgot about going to school. As all the children of the seaside village were going to school, Young-joo, all alone, went to the mountain behind the village.

The "mountain" was merely a name; it was only a hill, with a narrow pathway in the middle. The scenery on the opposite side was strikingly different. The left side of the hill boasted a place in the sun, blessed with woods composed of tall trees like oak and alder.

There was a tiny tomb on the sunny side. It must have been small from its beginning, as there was no evidence of soil being loosened by the weather. The cross, which was fixed in front of the tomb like a stake, had endured well through the years.

Young-joo sat down in front of the tomb and started to cry. "I don't know who you are, but if you come back to life, I know you'll be happy to play with me. Could you return to life? Would you, please?" She continued her heart-wrenching wailing but shed no tears to show how she truly felt.

"Am I not weeping enough to wake the child from death?" she asked herself. "When my father passed away last year, I saw a great number of people weep as sadly."

Ah, so many people swarmed into the house for her father's funeral, and every single person who came mourned sorrowfully. As they mourned, they looked more beautiful and more sincere than when she had previously seen them laughing and chattering. Then she felt that she did not dare to approach these adults. However, when she witnessed them wailing in grief, she was empathetic with them and felt she could help console their sorrow.

Young-joo was in high spirits on the day of her father's funeral. Very few people had come to see them since they had sought refuge at the seaside village after leaving their home in Seoul during the Korean War. Now, many people came, all wearing solemn expressions. How wonderful it was for her to have so many people there and plenty of food in the house.

Her older brother, who had left home after his marriage, was wearing a traditional funeral robe made from ramie fabric and a strange-looking headdress. He also carried a bamboo walking stick. He looked grotesquely unfamiliar, like a different person.

Young-joo wanted to have a bird's-eye view of the entire house, which was teeming with people. She went next door and climbed up on the stand that was built for holding huge storage jars. Content, she looked over the fence and witnessed her brother, attired in his strange mourning clothing, constantly bowing his head in her direction, and placing his hand on his walking stick. She was so overcome by his funny behavior that she nearly lost her balance and fell off the stand.

During the week of the funeral, Young-joo felt extremely important because of the abundance of everything throughout the house: people, food, and money. Her house seemed the best place in the whole neighborhood.

When people met her, they looked sympathetic and some declared, "Goodness gracious, we are most sorry for you, little one," or "When you get married, my dear, you'll miss your father so much." They spoke with tears in their eyes.

What a splendid and wonderful bier her father was carried in! Young-joo had never seen such a beautiful thing in the world before. The adults stuck money all around it. They believed the money would accompany her father and ensure his trip to the other world. Everyone was busy wailing their hearts out as if they were afraid of his return to this world if they did not cry enough. Even if her father wished to return, it would be improper for him to do so, especially after all these farewell arrangements.

But the death of this child in the little tomb was unlike any other, thought Young-joo. "The child must be sleeping now. After its long sleep, I am sure the child will ask me to play."

Young-joo climbed down the hill and went toward the village. There she summoned the little children, bored after their brothers and sisters went off to school for the day. Five little ones gathered around her. Leading those children, Young-joo again climbed the hill.

"Hey, you kids, you know how to wail for a dead person, don't you? You know, crying real sad; screaming and kicking when you cry. You have to cry just like that in front of this tomb, do you understand? Do you know that a child like you and me is in this tomb? Anyway, this child can come out alive if we cry a lot."

"How do you know if it's a child or an adult?" challenged one smart boy among the children.

"Because, don't you see, the tomb is small," said Young-joo.

"How can a dead person become alive? My grandmother said that the dead become ghosts."

"It's not true. You see, crying is like praying. If we cry with sincere hearts, this child in the tomb can return to life!"

"What is a prayer?"

"It is a heart without any lies."

"We already have enough living people around. What makes you think you need to revive the dead?" he retorted.

"You don't know what you're talking about. Do you know the only person who has no hatred or does not lie is the one who has come back to life after his death?"

"Do you really believe this child will return to life?" he challenged.

"Only if you and the other children weep hard," she replied.

"What if the dead one turns out to be a goblin?"

"Then, I will stay here alone. You and the other kids are free to go back to the village."

The children, who had listened in silence, started to cry in unison, in a mixture of different sounds and tones. Some knelt; others spread their arms wide, frowning deeply.

Young-joo clasped her hands and closed her eyes, thinking of how deeply she wished to see the child in the tomb. Lost completely in her thoughts, she began to shed real tears.

She opened her eyes slowly and cautiously after she had cried awhile. Bright sunlight entered through her narrowed eyelids. In the midst of this light, silver fluff was forming. This fluff was soaked by golden sunrays and emitted silvery light. The silvery light shimmered like a dancing figure floating over clear water. Overcome by this splendid sight, her eyes popped wide open.

Young-joo looked at the children crying around her. No tears ran down the cheeks of anyone. They merely pretended to be crying.

"Ah, the child in this tomb came as a willow bud! Because these kids would not believe, the tomb child felt too badly to come as it was!" Young-joo pondered.

"Well, kids," she said, "I can see you don't know how to weep. It's no use. Why don't you go back to the village?"

After her father's elaborate bier was removed, the house was more bleak than ever before. All the excitement vanished. Everything became frighteningly solemn. Her older brother and his wife returned to their home, and her mother left the house frequently on business. The children in the neighborhood stopped extending the special treatment that she had experienced during her father's funeral. People, in general, quickly forgot the mourning period of her father's death.

One day, Young-joo was skipping rope in the courtyard of her girlfriend, Kum-soon. Suddenly, the uncommon laughter of Kum-soon's sister and mother startled Young-joo. They were laughing so hard that tears rolled down their cheeks as they watched Young-joo, who was so absorbed in playing. Confused by their unusual laughter, she could not concentrate on skipping the rope properly. She looked down at herself. Previously, she had put a safety pin around the torn crotch of her pants; it was now flapping in a funny way, wide-open, below her knees.

"What kind of sister are you? Shame on you!" Kum-soon's mother stated, erasing her smile, and showing her displeasure.

"She's right, you know. How could you let your baby sister's hair become such a mess?" Kum-soon's older sister supported her mother's comment.

Young-joo sneaked away from the courtyard. She was ashamed of herself. Her pants had been in that shape for several days; her hair was messy all the time. What made Kum-soon's mother and sister make an issue of her appearance? Young-joo had never felt self-conscious before when they laughed at her. What did their laughter mean? "Why do I suddenly feel so strange about things which never bothered me before?" Young-joo wondered.

Upon returning home, she stood in front of the mirror. She studied her hair. It was weather-beaten and discolored by the sun and the salty air, tangled into a mess by the wind. Her sisters had completely neglected taking care of her hair.

"Good grief! Why, the texture of your hair is so fine, it is like silk thread. Once it tangles, it doesn't comb right." One of her sisters once made this comment. Young-joo's hair was as fine and smooth as silk then. Now it was dried and coarse, not shampooed often enough. Young-joo, who had been examining herself in front of the mirror, became sullen. She wondered what made the adults laugh at her appearance? Furthermore, the way they laughed was not pleasing to hear. She could detect a sense of shame in their laughter. Like poisonous smoke, the sense of shame permeated into her consciousness.

After she sent the children who didn't know how to wail sincerely back to the village, Young-joo went to a nearby stream and played all by herself around a willow tree. The willow tree was alive; so was the stream. The pebbles invited the stream to sing. The stream gurgled, given voice by the current that flowed around the stones. The pebbles tickled the current.

"Did you go to school today?" hounded Sun-joo, as soon as she came home from school in the evening. Sun-joo was wilted with exhaustion.

"Yes, I did. You're welcome to find out for yourself," lied Young-joo.

As she lay down in bed, Young-joo reassured herself, "Tomorrow I will go to that little tomb and tell the child that I lied to my sister about school. The child might understand why I had no choice but to lie. Tomorrow I will cry a lot alone by the tomb."

Coincidentally, the first anniversary of her father's death fell the day of her admission to elementary school. As if they were afraid of her father's return from death, the somber adults busied themselves taking Young-joo out of the school even before the opening ceremony was over. When her name was called by the homeroom teacher, they gave Young-joo enough time to answer, then took her home.

The following day when Young-joo went to school, she felt like an alien. On the previous day, the teacher must have handed out coloring paper to the new students right after the ceremony. With crayon, they were supposed to color either a flower or a house around a dotted line. The children who had received such materials now colored elaborately to the very best of their ability and displayed their pictures in high spirits. The teacher pretended not to see Young-joo in her class.

Young-joo had not only disliked the school but also feared it. The next day she skipped school. After a while, her family managed to discover her absence from school; it caused a great commotion in the house. Forcefully led by her mother, Young-joo went back to school. However, school was stranger than ever before.

Young-joo could not understand a single word that her teacher said. Her classmates seemed to understand everything. They responded with a "yes!", resembling baby swallows with their mouths open wide. Young-joo was the only one who could not participate.

"This wouldn't have happened to me if I had received coloring paper on the day of admission," thought Young-joo. No one in the family realized that after one mishap, many more would occur, one after another, making matters worse. Young-joo wondered why the adults felt compelled to pull her out of school that morning and take her home because of the ceremony commemorating her father's death, which was held that evening.

Now people in her neighborhood laughed at her, looking at her pants where the crotch was torn apart. They laughed at her dishevelled hair, whispering that it was like a coarse cushion. In school, her classmates snubbed her.

At home, things continued in the same dreary pattern, her mother away on business for ten days or even a fortnight; Moon-joo, spending all the money on self-adornment or snacks. The family was in debt. The housemaid continued to steal, and Sun-joo continued to tell the story about sticking a needle in the skin of a shelled, boiled egg.

"What makes people do what they do?" Young-joo wondered. She began to dislike people.

Under the hill where the train left from the town of Song-jong, turning inland and away from the sea, there was a gleaming white, blinding sandfield. Here the sun shown limitlessly until the sand radiated heat. The ocean became a dim light and held its breath. Blond-haired, blue-eyed women in blue or red bikinis covering only their private areas were sun-bathing, exposing their conspicuous fair white skin to the seethingly-hot, golden sand as they basked on the beach.

In the sea not far from the shore was a Swedish medical ship. The ship was white and huge, giving the impression of an ivory palace emerging from the blue sea. People said there was no poverty on that ship; it had everything; delicious foods, rare items, good quality clothing, warm people and wonderful medicine. They said the ship was equipped with all the things the villagers would never see. People also said it was like heaven. They took care of the patients, especially those who were wounded during combat. Once they were admitted, even the dead became resuscitated, people said. Those women who were basking in the golden sands were the nurses of the Swedish medical ship.

Young-joo frequently went upland where she could have a bird's-eye view of the white sandfield where the picture of the basking women unfolded. However, her interest only lasted for a few days. Nothing captivated her as much as weeping in front of that tiny tomb. "Did you go to school today?" her sister, Sun-joo, asked without fail every day. Although Sun-joo made it a habit to ask, she appeared to be just flapping her mouth, completely oblivious to the meaning of her question. Young-joo had to visit the tiny tomb everyday to confess lying to her sister.

As the sun lingered tiresomely longer, the air became hotter. The day was too long for Young-joo to play outside alone. "Are the waterbirds taking naps too? After carrying night beyond the horizon, they will come back after they've taken a good nap. The sun is taking its time, awaiting the waterbirds that flew away for their naps. . ." Young-joo thought. Anyway, her days were hot and boring. Likewise, weeping at the tomb became harder and hotter.

The bus, running hourly into the city, left nearly empty in the daytime. The noise of this antique bus running along the unpaved road was awful, but the terrible dust stirred up by the bus was worse. The village children threw themselves into the dust and tried their best to catch up with the bus. But this was not fun any more. At noontime, during this ferociously bright summer, the children wanted to hide from the excessive light and heat, but they had no place to go. Even the sun could not find the children as they plunged into the cloudy dust accompanied with the explosive sound of the bus. Yet, the dust did not swirl very long; it settled down soon.

One evening, Young-joo discovered an interesting sight right outside the village. Next to the chain of stores in the village was a Japanese-style wooden building. It had its own doorway, serving as both the entrance and exit; a woven-straw curtain hung upon it, reaching down to an adult's waist. From the outside, the floor of the room was clearly exposed. Through this door came a merry melody mingled with the beat of the crowd shouting "mambo, mambo!" or "samba, samba!"

The room was dense with shadows, lit by only one dim light. Legs moved langorously through the reddish light in a dancing motion. Since the upper part of their bodies could not be seen at all from outside, they looked like monsters with legs only.

The "mambo, mambo!, samba, samba!" that they sang sounded somehow sad to Young-joo, in spite of the heavy beat. She safely presumed that the smooth, bare legs belonged to girls and the others to men. She began to wonder if the women's legs might belong to those white women who lay on the golden sand-field at the beach near Song-jung village.

Sometimes different melodies sung in a charming lilt escaped under the curtain — "The hem of the pastel pink skirt flapping in the spring wind. . ." or, sung in a faster tempo, "Wearing a wide-rimmed straw hat sideways. . ." According to the melody, people either moved their legs fast or slowly crossed them, as if the tune exerted some magical spell over their movements.

The next morning Young-joo waited for her sisters to leave for school in their same boisterous manner. Then she stood in front of the mirror. She mimicked the sound of the melodies while she imitated the way people had moved their legs about on the previous night. However, it was not as appealing as weeping in front of the child's tomb.

One morning, Young-joo went back to the tomb, which was now choked with overgrown weeds. A startled snake slithered out of the weeds. Frightened, she rushed to the sandy beach out of breath and nearly collapsed. Trying to recover her breath, she gazed at the hazy horizon. Suddenly, her hand touched a wonderful-feeling, strange object. Greatly surprised, she looked down at her hand: a white, almost transparent, crumpled rubber pouch met her eyes. It was partially buried in the wet sand near the tideline, as if it were trying to hide. Young-joo picked the object up and went to the well. It was quiet near the well at noontime. The well-site, which was all muddy in the mornings and evenings, had now been dried white as if bleached under the strong afternoon sunlight. On her tip-toes, Young-joo drew water from the well in a bucket. She washed the thin, rubber pouch very carefully lest she harm it. She believed it would make an excellent balloon. She was elated. Someone was standing behind her, giggling. She turned around to look, feeling ill-at-ease. It was the oldest brother of her girlfriend, Ja. He worked for the American military outfit.

"Hey, where did you find that thing?"

"On the beach," Young-joo answered.

"Do you know what that is?" he asked.

"It's a balloon."

"Balloon?" Ja's brother cackled as if his whole stomach was itching. Young-joo sank into inexplicable embarassment. She was ashamed of her hands that had been washing the balloon.

Ja's brother opened his mouth, still cackling.

"Hey, why don't you try wailing, putting your mouth on that thing?"

"Wailing is for the dead!" Young-joo said loudly since she was embarrassed.

"That's right, my dear. What you have in your hand is like a tomb where a baby has been killed and buried," he giggled.

Young-joo sprang to her feet. Her face turning crimson, she shouted to him. "Don't you lie!"

"What makes you think I'd lie to you? You ask your sisters. Then you'll know. Ask your oldest sister," he said, still giggling.

Ja's brother kept on mumbling and stretching his neck. He left, singing a song that didn't make any sense. Young-joo crouched on the ground again and finished washing the thing.

"A tomb of a dead child who was my age? Did he mean that this is a tomb? Someone of my age has died?" Young-joo pondered.

She shook off the moisture from the rubber pouch, tilting her head. As if she were trying to find a child in it, Young-joo opened its mouth and looked inside. Then she put her mouth onto the cleanly washed pouch and put air into it with all her strength.

The balloon grew larger and larger, becoming more transparent. After she tightly tied the top part with a string of thread, it floated off into the sky. The small children in the village gathered around her, making exclamations of "Wow". At that moment, Young-joo was the queen of the day.

Summer vacation for her two older sisters freed Young-joo from her task of making seaweed-wrapped rice. She also was able to relax from her going-to-school business. On top of it all, she managed to make another new discovery. If she went out to the sandy beach near the suspected American military corps, she could pick up several such balloons at one time. Young-joo didn't bother to share her secret about the balloons with the village children. She did not follow through on the advice given by Ja's brother regarding the balloons either. She couldn't put her finger on it, but somehow her intuition told her she had no business asking her sister about the balloons as Ja's brother advised. Therefore, before she returned home, Young-joo tied the balloon that she had been playing with during the day on a low branch of a tree in the woods where the child's tomb was located.

Young-joo became decisively popular among the village children. She was the "queen of the white balloons." As a consequence of following the balloons as they rose upward in the air, the children's necks became stiff. Young-joo took pleasure in watching the balloons. She enjoyed being the center of attention. The children continuously gathered around her each day.

She often slept fitfully as dawn approached due to her desire to go out to the seaside, if she could, before the waterbirds left, carrying the darkness in their beaks. She did not want any of the kids to find "one" on the beach.

However, for some unknown reason, the waterbirds left the sea too early, taking the residual darkness with them. Moreover, they abandoned the sun far too late in the sky, driving it into exhaustion by staying so long in the summer air.

Young-joo always dashed to the beach in a flurry. She could not afford to allow any of her peers to spot "one" lying on the sandy beach.

She did not take a balloon to the well-site anymore. Instead, she went alone to the stream by the tomb and washed it. Then she blew into it until her face turned scarlet. At the very moment when it was touched by her own breath, the rubber pouch came to life. Before then, it had been nothing but a soft and powerless object, crumpled and formless. When it had all the air inside that it could hold, the balloon produced a whining noise as if it were saying "no more, no more." Then it floated upward to the sky.

When evening descended, Young-joo set free the balloon with which she had been playing during the daytime. The village children stomped their feet and yelled out of sincere regret that she had released the balloon. The deeper the children showed their feelings of regret, the more adamant Young-joo became about setting the balloon free.

When the stars came out in the night sky, Young-joo went alone outside in the front courtyard and gazed up at the sky. "Which star is the balloon that I set free? Which star has it reached?" she wondered.

The next day, Young Joo, who had been with the village children by the child's tomb, was seized with a sudden desire to fly.

"Who can blow the best among you?" Young-joo asked.

"Me, me," each and every child came forward, raising his hand. Strong boys pushed the girls aside. The leader of the boys, who was in the second grade, shouted: "The strongest one must have the strongest lungs, you see!"

"If that's so, can you blow air into my mouth just like blowing the balloon?" she asked.

"Good grief, you terrible girl! That's kissing like the grownups do. Do you want me to kiss you?" the boy cackled.

The way the boy giggled was exactly the way Ja's brother had laughed at Young-joo. She became angry.

"Who said anything about kissing me? I was talking about blowing in air!"

"What are you going to do, then, with the air?" the boy asked.

"Forget it! I'm not going to talk to you anymore," Young-joo cried.

"Why is kissing so bad?" Young-joo wondered. Yet, she didn't bother to challenge the boy. She decided not to ask the boy to blow air into her mouth again. In this mood, Young-joo came up with an excuse that would cause the children to leave. She waited as they left, picking the most docile and well-behaved girl to stay behind with her.

When Young-joo was left alone with the girl, she laid down flat, right in front of the child's tomb. Then she asked the girl, "Will you try to blow air into my mouth? While I leave it open, you blow air with all your might."

The girl hesitated for a good while before she bent from her waist towards Young-joo. Then, the girl followed Young-joo's request to blow air into her mouth until her face turned red.

It was at that very moment that a group of boys, who had been hiding under the shade in the dark woods across the stream, jumped up. In unison, they screamed "wa."

Young-joo was pulled into the house by her oldest sister.

"You wretched girl! Do you have any idea what it is that you're making a balloon from?" her sister said in great irritation, pushing her in front of her mother who happened to be home.

"Look at this girl, mother. She is such a naughty girl, doing all sorts of terrible things. Listen to this, Mom. She has been picking these dirty things off the beach and making them into balloons," her sister explained. "That revolting guy, Ja's older brother, has been teasing me whenever I happen to pass him, implying that I taught Young-joo a good thing. I wasn't sure what he meant by that. Oh, my word, this miserable war is even ruining children..."

"My daughter, there are not many people who are enduring the war as easily as we have been," her mother said. "Why don't you leave your baby sister alone? That poor child of mine! Don't you see she is not under my wing and has not one toy to play with. She must be awfully bored."

"Oh, my dear mother!" Her oldest daughter gave up, her mouth hanging wide open.

As the new school year approached, the waterbirds, which flew to bring back darkness, returned a little earlier than before. Young-joo's sisters made a great fuss, as usual, around breakfast time. After such commotion was over, Young-joo could enjoy her freedom.

School snatched her entire group of peers from her. Young-joo pulled the children, who were on their way to school, to her side. She tried to tempt them by offering a balloon. She stole some of her sisters' nice belongings to lure the children away from school. Quite a few children took her bait. Some threw their school backpacks into the woods and rushed to the seaside; some played by the child's tomb.

However, this affair was short-lived. One day, a child went back to school crying, after he recovered his school backpack. On that same afternoon, his teacher, holding his hand, came to the site where they had been playing. The rest of the children, all in a group, went back to school, led by the teacher. Like an inmate, Young-joo was dragged to school, too.

"Who told you children not to go to school? Who was the first to suggest it?" the teacher questioned. Young-joo was the last one to be interrogated. She was taken to the classroom and punished. She went to school to be punished, not to learn.

While she was standing for her punishment, she could over-hear the children whispering.

"I heard that she lives in front of a tomb," someone whispered.

"I heard she was possessed by the spirit of a dead child," the other said.

Among those mumuring children, Young-joo could spot a few who had been playing with her not long ago. She did not cry. "I can cry as much as I want in front of the tomb. Why then, should I cry here?" She neither shut her eyes nor bent her head. "Even if I keep my eyes open, you children, I'm not looking at you. I alone see the tomb, blow the balloons, and go out to find the waterbirds," she thought.

As autumn was ushered in, the ease of picking up balloons at the seaside waned. Not a single one could be found, no matter how carefully she searched. Young-joo went to school every day, dragged by a village child from the second grade class. Nevertheless, near the gathering of dusk, she went out to the evening sea to meet the waterbirds that would bring the darkness with them.

As the waterbirds returned, carrying darkness, Young-joo paid no attention to the murmurings of the village folks. The whisperings of the children faded away. She believed that she was the only soul who understood it was the waterbirds that came to open the gate of morning.

The fact that she knew this pleased her.

Translated by Hyun-jae Yee Sallee

PURCHASED BRIDEGROOM

BY ICK-SUH YOO

I do not want the story of this period of my life to be widespread. How shameful and humiliating that would be! In spite of my wishes, however, my affairs have already become common knowledge among quite a number of people. The story took place in the home of the president of a company who must have had at least three hundred employees working for him. The story has been spread not only among the company employees and their acquaintances, but even among my friends.

When the story was first heard within the company, the employees whispered, and as if it were a public debate, they divided into two groups. One group felt sorry for me; the other sneered at me. The jeerers overwhelmingly outnumbered the sympathizers, of whom there was only a handful.

Those who had secretly been scornful of my actions from the beginning, when I had taken the handicapped daughter of the president as my wife and had begun living at my in-laws' home, must have been pleased to see how badly it turned out. I even believe that those few people who sympathized with me did not do so out of any genuine concern for my well-being. It was really nothing to them but idle talk. How in the world, they asked one another, could such a thing possibly happen? They enjoyed coming to some conclusion about the merits of how I had been treated by my in-laws.

Even that handful of sympathizers, however, turned their backs on me in the end and sneered at me. They might have experienced a change of heart had they paused to realize that one can never expect anything in this life. Reminded by that thought, they might have been inclined to believe the proverb that undoubtedly a pine caterpillar lives properly by eating pine leaves only.

Today, I am far, far away from those people. Right after the whole thing fell apart, I fled from my in-laws as fast as a wife caught having sex with her lover. I have never gone back there, not even once, wishing my wife and her parents would completely forget me and erase any thoughts of me from their minds.

Yes, it has been five years now since it all happened. I have tried to heal my pain in every way. Yet, it still stays with me even after these five years have elapsed. How many more years will it take for my pain to go, I wonder. People say that time marks the face of a man as it will without his knowing. Is not five years sufficient time to heal this hurt? I would like to believe such a span of time is enough to heal my wounds. I shudder at the thought that I may carry this pain to my grave.

I am terribly conscious of my story being widely known. Then, what makes me reveal it now? If I am forced to produce reasons, I have two. One is an urge to explain once and for all to those who sneer at me. I have no idea how the story about me could possibly have followed me so far. Lately, I have been the subject of other's conversation quite often. The other reason is an earnest wish to forget by sorting out my experience from the beginning to the end, hoping it will help me escape from the memories, as I desperately long to do.

I regret that these two reasons really are inadequate to serve as an excuse for disclosing everything. But what can I do? If the rumors about me were based on nothing but truth, I would not have to resort to this method. Unfortunately, people are sneering at me more and more as each day progresses. Vicious rumors have a way of becoming transformed as they are transmitted, and the vicious changes being made as the story passes from mouth to mouth are more than I can ignore. For this reason, I voluntarily decided to unveil my story exactly as it happened. I only wish that this story not be transformed into something so grotesque that it is unrecognizeable.

If only I had a distant relative, or a first cousin on either parent's side, that relative might have heard my appeal, starting with the phrase "how in the world could something like this happen?" I don't know whether I'm fortunate or not, but I did not even have one single distant relative who might have lent a sympathetic ear to my problem. Some of my friends were entertained by my problem; others merely warned me that one can easily get hurt if he gets involved with someone of a higher class, forgetting his own humble origins. That's the way the world is made, they said. There are different social classes.

I am not implying that all of my friends fell into these categories. I must say that I had one good friend who shared my pain and suffered along with me. We met much more often because I needed him. We first knew each other in high school and quickly became fast friends. He became my regular consultant out of a sense of obligation because of our friendship. He knew everything in detail, from the start to the end. He shared my joy at first and then carried the burden of anger when it turned bad. When my marriage ended, he was as disturbed as I was, shuddering violently, overcome with rage.

I barely managed to graduate from college, and then I served in the Army. After finishing my tour with the army, I looked for a job. When I remember those days, I feel as if every hair on my head could turn white. To find employment, I covered the streets of the town all day long, while my thoughts covered a thousand miles each day. Every evening I returned in a ragged mood to the dark room that I rented. Then, when my future seemed to be hopelessly dim, I finally landed a job. My best friend was as jubilant as I at the news, as if he had landed the job himself.

After three months with the company, I was able to tell my friend I was getting married to the crippled daughter of the company president. His reaction was overwhelmingly practical. Before I finally agreed to the marriage, I had been worn to a fray by the president and his wife for ten days and ten sleepless nights. They had tempted me with everything they could think of. My friend, who didn't know what I'd been through, was happy for me, thinking it would ease my hard and lonely life. He saw my proposed marriage as sweet rain coming down after a drought. I had been utterly exhausted by my future in-laws' description of a future filled with every pleasure available in the world.

"Please think of it as getting married to us rather than to our daughter," the president said.

His wife tried a different lure. "You must have had a hard life. I am moved by the fact that you supported yourself through college. I imagine quite a few of you young men felt abandoned after the Korean War. But now it's your turn to get ahead. Please have courage and accept it."

At last they succeeded in winning me over by using such enticement, and I found myself taking the lure. I admitted to myself, though, that greed for their money was the main reason I was consenting to marry their daughter. My spirits were as dampened as a straw mat during the rainy season. If I had to calculate the motive for my consent by percentages, seventy percent, quite over half, was the exhaustion of a young man who was sick and tired of being poverty-stricken. However, I did feel sorry for them because they were so anxious to have someone marry their daughter, who was a chronic invalid. The pity I felt for them was about ten percent. Another ten percent was just plain hopeless-ness. I didn't believe I could possibly be any more miserable with a handicapped person as my wife than I already was. The final ten percent was comprised of various reasons, mostly trivial.

During the time they were trying their utmost to win over my heart into marrying their daughter, I perceived their pitiful posi-tion. The money that they had was the result of a desperate struggle; they had diligently sacrificed, neglecting rest and proper food in their determination to become rich. I even sympathized with their hope of finding a suitable son-in-law who would take care of their crippled child. What if the wrong kind of man mar-ried their daughter? After their deaths, he could take their entire estate for his own then desert her. If that happened, she might wander the streets and become as thin as a wisp of straw and finally starve to death. I could tell that these were major con-cerns.

It is clear now what might have prompted them to choose me as a fitting person for their daughter. I was vulnerable and did not have a single relative. Careful consideration of me on their part and greed for money on my part finally brought us to an agreement. At this moment, however, another idea crept into my mind. Even if I, blinded by greed, took a crippled woman as my wife, might we not lead as happy a life as many normal married couples? On the other hand, I reasoned, if it didn't turn out well, the sooner I met my fate the better.

When I disclosed this shameful agreement to my friend, he extended immediate congratulations. Although I have no certain proof of his thoughts, I felt he was not truly happy, for my sake, about this marriage. I was certain, though, that he was excited over this chance for me to, at least, have money. And I believe he paid me the compliment of believing that I possessed some prac-tical sense. Whatever his motives, he treated me to drinks and made a great fuss. As I look back in my present mood of loneli-ness, I find myself now dismissing his friendly gestures.

However, when a second chance came for my friend to congratulate me, I received his congratulations with real pleasure. This was two years after my marriage, as a son-in-law now living with my wife and her parents. My crippled wife, who had been confined to a wheelchair, was transformed into a normal woman with healthy legs after an operation. What happened to my wife was an amazing, miraculous thing that might occur only in fairy tales.

My married life had been as perilous as walking a tight rope. The hardest thing for me was being afraid to express my feelings. Having a crippled wife depressed me. I did not experience even a single bright day. My spirit was as damp as if rain were falling inside me. Mentally, I felt constricted. I wished to conceal my inner feelings at any cost; consequently, I was nervous all the time. But being rather sly, I was able to behave in such a way as to keep my inner turmoil a secret.

Whenever I was with my in-laws, I was careful of everything I did or said. I tried to remain taciturn, constantly concealing a smoldering inner anger at my situation, such as a person might feel living through great hardships. I am sure they were glad, after all, to have a son-in-law too timid and foolish to confront them with his true feelings.

My mother-in-law wore a tireless smile on her face whenever she looked at me. She even tried to flatter me with flowery remarks intended to soothe my feelings.

"After marrying you, she's become a new person, beyond recognition," my mother-in-law would coo in an effort to bind me and my wife together.

In spite of my mother-in-law's efforts, however, I greatly disliked the smell that came from my wife. She involuntarily spread an odor of sickness in the air. I suffered nightmares because of this. I dreamed that I was sleeping with a cold-blooded animal in my arms. Undoubtedly, there was warm blood running through her veins, but only after touching her could I be assured of this. Her pale face was like wax; her eyes were always large as if greatly surprised. Her breasts were under-developed; her white fingers were long and creepy. Moreover, her legs dangled independently of each other, controlled neither involuntarily or by her will. All this made each night long and agonizing for me.

I had to make an effort to refrain from using abusive language when I approached her sexually. This happened infrequently, as my wife couldn't bear the pain that a normal sexual position caused in her hip joints. For this reason, I had to make love to her while she was lying on her side. Having unsatisfactory sex in such an uncomfortable position, I usually had to finish myself off after I satisfied my wife's physical needs. Whether or not she guessed my inner thoughts, my wife seemed to be intoxicated with happiness.

Finally, my wife became pregnant. She was beside herself with joy; she was ready to fly upward to the sky. Her parents were as ecstatic as she was. I questioned whether the news of any woman's pregnancy truly deserved such an overwhelming amount of excitement.

Unfortunately, their rapture did not last very long. A family doctor, who made a house call to take care of my wife when she caught a cold, announced that she should give up any hope of a full-term pregnancy. Her physical strength was not sufficient to support a pregnancy. She was, by that time, nearly three months pregnant. The entire household was immediately plunged into darkness by the doctor's unexpected diagnosis. Another doctor who was summoned strongly recommended an abortion. Before he left, he said that my wife's life might be threatened if she did not abort early enough.

My dismay surpassed the disappointment of my wife's parents and even my wife. Once I had a child of my own, I could antici-pate days filled with love and joy. My expectations for such hap-piness were now shattered into a thousand pieces. After that, my wife stubbornly carried the baby for two more months. She had an abortion at the university hospital.

From her first day in the hospital, my wife could not stop cry-ing. After a while, though, her sorrowful weeping made me angry. Having to abort the baby might well have caused her to be one of the unhappiest people in the world at that particular time, but ceaseless weeping was more than I could handle.

After the operation, my wife had to stay in the hospital for a few more days due to her weak condition. Little by little, her grief began to subside. Whenever I was in her room, she would merely gaze at me, her large eyes filled with shame.

One day, while she was still in the hospital, the doctor in charge announced something quite extraordinary. He said there might be a way for my wife's deformity to be corrected. He advised us to take my wife to an orthopedic doctor for an examination, no matter what the diagnosis might turn out to be. All of us were keyed up at his suggestion.

Upon receiving this advice, my wife's parents suddenly became flustered. They were as anxious as if the treasure in their hands might be lost by a single wrong move. At every opportunity, my in-laws asked questions about anything and everything having to do with the possibility of a cure. The sorrow of my wife's inescapable abortion was quickly forgotten, and we found ourselves blossoming with new hope for her.

At last, the diagnosis of her case was pronounced.

"She was born with a dislocated hip joint. I can't guarantee anything, but it's just possible it can be corrected by an operation. We may be able to restore the dislocated joint to its normal position."

"Can this be true?" my mother-in-law cried in amazement at the doctor's statement. "Oh, something like this was always possible for you, my dear. We were so ignorant that we had no idea." My mother-in-law threw herself into her daughter's arms and burst into tears.

My father-in-law was also overwhelmed.

The doctor said, "After you regain your strength, you can have the operation."

We were speechless. That night my wife only cried, clinging tightly to me.

My wife had two major orthopedic operations. She stayed in the hospital for another two months. After a routine checkup, she was ready to be discharged from the hospital as a normal, healthy person.

For the first time in my life, I realized that one tends not to appreciate many things while he strives madly to cope with misfortune befalling him. Is it because misfortune makes one see things differently?

The evening when I heard the glad news of my wife's successful surgery, I gazed at the moon as if for the first time and appreciated its beauty with newly-found joy. For the first time, I woke up to the warmth of the moonlit world, trees, walls, roofs, and mountains resting comfortably in the distance, these appealed to my newly-opened eyes. I was sad that the moon waned as the night passed and disappeared when morning neared. Even so, I felt as if I were reborn.

My best friend at once cheerfully volunteered to buy me a drink after he heard the story about my wife's operation. While drinking, he made such comments as "Your round, jovial face suggests you're blessed with good luck" or "There is an adage that goes like this: 'A gold statue decorated with flowers. . .' As it is, my friend, you have been doubly blessed with a beautiful wife and impressive wealth" or "You must feel like you're in a dream."

He continued to make such remarks in a flattering manner. Moreover, he seemed ten times happier than I. Affected by him, I cheerfully seconded his comments. I drank with him far into the night, continuing to receive his congratulatory remarks.

However, when my best friend and I met for the third time, we sat facing each other across the table; we remained mute, only expelling deep sighs in a gloomy mood. This time I bought him drinks that tasted bitter. My friend either nodded his head or frowned at my story while he gulped down wine. "How in the world could such a thing possibly happen!" He blurted out this exclamatory remark every once in a while. At that particular point in my life, I was driven into a desperate situation. I faced a problem that offered no alternative but to leave my wife's house. I was at the end of my rope. That was when I called upon my friend, whom I regarded as a "confidant," to share my dilemma. At that time, every morning I girded myself with the firm conviction that I must resolve my problem once and for all. When evening descended, however, I found myself lacking the courage to carry out the plan. I blamed my incompetence. It was during those days that I saw him again.

As I mentioned earlier, the success of my wife's operation brought me an overwhelming sense of happiness. Was it due to my exceeding happiness that I missed the change? I had not noticed the slightest sign of her parents' scheming, although I was not allowed to see my wife after her operation. According to her physician, my wife required absolute rest. Consequently, I believed this was why I was not allowed to visit her. I even enjoyed some peace of mind, convinced I would see her as soon as she recovered her health. There was no need, therefore, for me to be fretful and anxious about her. Besides, my head was crowded with plans for the new life my wife and I would now enjoy.

"She's changed considerably. She's gained some weight. She looks so pretty with her flushed complexion." "She's no longer her old self. Her speedy recovery is a lot faster than expected. Yesterday, she even took a few steps." "I'm not saying this to you just because she's my daughter, but it's rare to find beauty such as hers in this world." In this fashion, my mother-in-law would deliver the news of my wife. Then her usual garrulous nature disappeared, and she tried to satisfy my waiting ears with fewer and fewer words.

For some unknown reason, my mother-in-law would sink into a melancholy mood after she would tell me about my wife. I simply thought such happiness must have overpowered her, making her pensive. I never once sensed their secret plot.

I only began to suspect something after I learned that my wife had left for the remote countryside immediately after being discharged from the hospital and would remain there to recuperate.

I could not understand her actions. Why wouldn't she see her husband, who had been waiting and waiting for her return? To make matters worse, why did she go on such a trip, using recuperation as an excuse?

I asked my mother-in-law the reason for my wife's conduct.

"I urged her to see you before she left, but she seemed to be in such a hurry!" My mother-in-law gave me the impression my wife was avoiding me. From that day on, I began to suspect my wife. One suspicion led to another. These suspicions led to other suspicions of a different shape and form. In the end, the entire world was filled with nothing but endless suspicions.

Each and every day, I found myself scrutinizing my suspicions. I once heard a story about a prisoner who could see nothing but the sky from his cell. He would imagine different things every day just by gazing at the unchanging sky. Then he was happy, sad, or despairing according to what he imagined. By the same token, I became enraged, anxious, or fretful by regarding my suspicions, as if they were confined in a transparent glass box.

No one, not my mother-in-law, not my father-in-law, not my wife, helped ease the suspicions I created. Whenever she saw me, my mother-in-law would deliberately avoid my eyes as a sly, hundred-year-old fox might hide its tail under its legs. My father-in-law would make a sheepish, false cough whenever I was around him. He would also pucker his lips in discomfort. Now, not a single item of news reached me from my wife.

One and then two months passed without any news from her. I knew my in-laws were aware of what was going on with their daughter, yet they never showed the slightest indication that they knew. Finally, I got a hint that the situation between me and my wife was final. Being aware of this, it was more awkward than ever for me to ask or demand explanations. Somehow, I felt I was opening my own wound if I asked questions about my wife. Because of this feeling, the atmosphere at the breakfast table, the only time of day my in-laws and I were able to be together, was as awkward as trying to assemble a shattered porcelain bowl by force. Their plotting increased daily. Merciless pressure was exerted on me, the person in the middle.

Then one morning, I discovered a sudden change in our breakfast schedule. When I went down to the dining room, I learned that my father-in-law had already eaten breakfast and left for work, and my mother-in-law was still in bed, complaining of a headache. After that particular morning, I did not even have an opportunity to see their faces anymore. On top of that, when I came home from work that day, I found my possessions had been moved to a different location. The bedroom my wife and I had shared was cleaned out completely.

I went upstairs, following the housemaid into the main part of the house and past my in-laws. As the maid opened the door of the new room for me, some violent force surged through my heart, and my eyes were blurred with dizziness. From that day on, I slept in that room, furnished only with a bed and a cheap vinyl dresser.

Something that helped me see the whole matter in its true light took place several days after my room had been changed. It confirmed my suspicions concerning their secret plot against me. A letter from my wife was waiting for me when I came home.

"I've decided to put everything behind me and make a fresh start with my life," it read. "Please try to understand my decision and find it in your heart to forgive me. . . Wish you happiness always. . ."

What else could I do after reading my wife's letter? What path should I take? Without a doubt, the wisest thing for me to do was to leave my wife's house quietly. After all, I had suffered a great deal by now. I was so choked with the feeling of loss that I crumbled the letter and ran downstairs, stomping in rage. I demanded an explanation of what in heaven's name was going on, thrusting the letter right under my mother-in-law's nose. For a little while, she appeared to be uncomfortable; she could not hide her embarrassment. Then, as if she had made up her mind to act, my mother-in-law changed her attitude entirely, playing the innocent.

"I haven't the faintest notion what's going on. How can I possibly know her innermost thoughts?"

I pressed her with determination, in a tone of disgust, recalling every different kind of humiliation that I had received and endured. Yet, my mother-in-law was immovable. I fell into low spirits.

For the first time, I realized how unshakeable they were. I had no choice but to withdraw myself, greatly discouraged. I was also enveloped with an overwhelming sense of despair upon realizing that a decision had already been made as to who was going to be the victor and who the defeated.

Two days after that confrontation with my mother-in-law, my wife returned home. I knew this because there was a pair of unfamiliar shoes in the front entrance hall. Besides the physical evidence, I could also feel a different air permeating the entire house. When I implicitly asked the maid, she confirmed it just as expected. Still, my wife did not show herself in my presence.

Two or three days elapsed after her return. I could not stand it any longer, and I went downstairs searching for my wife in order for us to have a final talk. My mother-in-law, however, blocked my way, informing me that my wife had not returned home from her afternoon outing.

Another week passed. I could not find her anywhere in the house. I was under the impression that she and her parents were just waiting for me to leave their house of my own will because of my dampened spirits. Their waiting attitude was as tenacious and persistent as that of a stubborn woman.

"Their plot must have already been formed when her operation was performed," my friend said, following his remark with a mouthful of bitter wine. I drank as my friend did, bitterly. "Now, my friend," he continued, "you're no longer good enough for the normal, healthy daughter of the company president. It looks that way, doesn't it? In other words, it seems to me, you're not needed any longer."

After he made this remark, my friend and I took another drink, at the same time, with a kindred thirst. I continued to nod my head at his words. "Yes, my friend, you've been carrying a 'Nak-dong River duck' in your arms!"

"What do you mean?" I asked.

"What I mean is that you have assumed the role of poor mother hen for your wife."

Although I did not have the faintest idea what he was referring to, I kept nodding my head.

"I hate to say this, my friend, but you'd be better off to leave that house as soon as possible."

"I suppose there's no other choice left for me. But their behavior is uncalled for!" I cried.

"I know how you feel, my friend. However, what are you going to do about it? The ducklings have swum away."

Again, I was completely lost at his remark.

"What! You've never heard that story? Well, then, I'll tell you," my friend said. "There was a mother hen who didn't know that the eggs she was sitting on were duck eggs. Anyway, she took good care of them. The eggs hatched and ducklings came out. One day when the ducklings were strong enough to move around freely, they jumped into the water one by one. Watching them plunge into the water, the mother hen was terrified. She didn't know what to do. She ran around in great anxiety, staying on the bank. She was helpless since she couldn't jump into the water. The gliding ducklings, sailing in high spirits, glanced back stealthily. 'It's too bad, don't you agree?' one duckling remarked. 'I know, but, there's nothing we can do about it. We can't spend our lives staying on the bank,' grumbled another. 'We feel sorry for our mother hen,' the third responded, 'but we must forget her.' After that conversation among the ducklings, they all disappeared, gliding leisurely away."

As I listened to the story, I nodded my head and muttered suspiciously. "Then my wife was that hateful duckling!"

"In any event, my friend, don't just leave without anything. You need to summon your nerve in order to receive a fat alimony from them," my friend said, not forgetting to give me a piece of advice.

I did not, however, receive even a penny from them as alimony or consolation money, despite my friend's advice. For no good reason, led only by an indescribable impulse, I left my wife's house in despair, taking only her wheelchair that had been placed against the wall out by the storage shed. The wheelchair that my wife had formerly used represented a part of her body. During her hospitalization, it had been kept carefully in our room. One day, however, it was suddenly dragged outside and then left uncared for by the shed. Since then, it had rained and snowed, yet the wheelchair was not carried inside. Whenever I saw the wheelchair, I reminded myself that it should be put away somewhere in the shed. Yet, I kept forgetting to carry out my intention.

Anyway, I left my wife's house in a dispirited mood, with only a rusted wheelchair, which I pushed. I will never forget the shame I felt on that day. I was gloomy, foolish, preposterous, and irresolute. On that day, I was transformed into an obvious mental cripple.

On that particular day, I came home earlier than usual with the idea in mind that in any event I must make a decision. I came prepared with nothing but a tarnished fruit knife that I purchased after much hesitation at a general store on my way home.

Lately, I had felt that the front gate seemed to frown at me whenever I faced it, as if rebuking my lowly position in the household. It had already turned its face from me. This uncomfortable daily feeling induced the extravagant notion that if I owned a house, it would have an unlocked gate at the front that could be opened from outside by merely pushing on it. It was nothing but an idle wish. Every other household had a similar locked gate with the same intercom device so that it could be opened only from the inside. It was a one-sided decision as far as opening the gate was concerned. Before long, that gate would not be opened for me anymore. Yes, starting tomorrow for sure, I told myself.

Spurred on by this thought, I glared at the ivory doorbell, as small as my wife's nipples, which had stopped developing due to the lack of suckling. Feeling a severe sense of thirst, I pushed the doorbell. My fingers had become pitifully thin in recent months. As soon as I had pushed the doorbell, I immediately put my hand into my pocket. I touched the fruit knife that I had bought before I came home. An acute chill ran from my finger tips to my heart.

"Who is it?" came a voice over the intercom.

I was taken aback at the inquiry from inside. I had completely forgotten that I had rung the doorbell.

"It's me," I answered, feeling a streak of cold sweat down my spine. Although the gate was opened for me, I stood there absent-mindedly for a while. I felt an urgency to hide the fruit knife somewhere before I entered. Realizing that there were no other proper places for me to hide it except inside my pocket, I hastily stepped inside.

As I walked inside the entrance hall, my eyes quickly looked for my wife's shoes. I could not find them anywhere. I wondered if she might have put her shoes in a cupboard. Something from the past suddenly flashed sadly through my mind. My wife always used to wait for my return home from work, sitting in her wheelchair on this same wooden floor in the entrance hall. She would wear a smile on her face that was almost emotionless. Well, that seemed to have been a long, long time ago.

The mood of the entire house was quiet, as if not even one particle of dust shifted in the air.

"Is any one home?" I asked the maid.

"Everyone is here."

"Everyone" referred to my wife and my mother-in-law. With the housemaid's answer, my mind prepared itself with determination. Like a rock in a dark shadow, my mind grew more solid.

Alas! That state of mind did not last long. When I went upstairs and stood in front of my room, my resolution started to crumble again. I did not have the slightest idea why the doorknob suddenly reminded me of my wife's face. The shining stainless steel doorknob seemed to challenge me with an arrogant start, just as my wife's face would have. My wife had already taken the key away from me and had learned to unlock the door of her own world.

Even if I were armored with the firmest resolution to pursue my plan, my wife would not be affected. She would remain as firm as the earth. As I thought of this, I lost all hope again. An idea crept into my mind that my room might already be locked too. Hurriedly I grabbed the knob and twisted it. Mocking my fears, the door opened quite easily although the effort had brought sweat out on my forehead. At that very moment, I fell into despondency, and my energy was sapped. As soon as I walked into my room, I plopped down on the bed.

"You're right. You can't put it off any longer. You can't afford to wait anymore. A winner and a loser have already been decided in this fight." Repeatedly I said these words to myself. Regardless of my thoughts, I found myself getting weaker and weaker. I knew that they would not ask me to leave. They would wait patiently until I left them of my own accord after they had eroded my endurance. They would calculate the longest period of time that I could possibly hold out. Yes, it was evident that they were surely mean-spirited, having decided that a weak person would so readily give in out of discouragement. Yes, they had figured it out all right. I could not tolerate this situation anymore. As they would have me do, I made up my mind once and for all.

Suddenly, I felt the weight of the fruit knife in my pocket. I took it out. The tarnished, silver-toned, stainless-steel fruit knife bore a gloomy look. A fruit knife, almost twenty-five centimeters long, lay with no will of its own in my palm. When the owner's will was transmitted to the knife, then it would play a definite role accordingly, I surmised. The knife would obey without fail the will of its user, even to a ray of light being reflected. I shook my head when I remembered my thoughts at the time of purchasing the knife. Fearing that my will might be thwarted, fearing that I might be weakening again, I had bought this fruit knife, a destructive weapon. Yes, the thought of carrying a deadly weapon with me, I had hoped, might drive me into brutal action.

Even at the time when I purchased the knife, I feared it would never play the role of a murderous weapon. It was apparent that any kind of a deadly weapon would lose its power once it rested in my hand. It was true that such a thought was taking shape even while I made the purchase. Subconsciously, I made the deliberate choice of buying a blunt stainless-steel knife instead of a sharp-edged, intimidating one. Could I, in any way, defeat them even if I fought? Would they respond even if I demanded an explanation?

Suddenly, my wife's pet cat, Nabi, who had once held all of my wife's love, came into my mind. Nabi's fur was mixed with black and white, in an attractive pattern. The tip of her nose was pink. With my wife confined to her bed or in her wheelchair, the cat had been her most loved, playful, animate toy.

Last winter, however, this cat had been thrown out into the cold. Because of an extremely trivial act, the cat had incurred my wife's hatred as cold as frost. Truly, truly, Nabi must not have done it intentionally. I was told that she had walked across a shirt of mine which had been laid out for me to wear to work the next morning. My wife believed that this would bring bad luck. Since I wasn't there when it happened, I found out about it only after I came home from work.

It was quite strange that Nabi wasn't to be seen anywhere when I got home from work that day. When I asked my wife the whereabouts of the cat, she informed me Nabi had been kicked out of the house because of what she had done. Half-jokingly, I tried to beg forgiveness for Nabi. My attempt proved futile. Perhaps due to her handicap, my wife had no spirit of forgiveness and could not change once her heart was hardened.

Nabi could not understand my wife's detesting her. On the night that Nabi was thrown out, we slept fitfully due to the cat's meowing by the window all night long. The next night was even worse. Nabi scratched on the wall. As if she were a messenger from Hell, she made a shivering, moaning sound which sent chills up our spines.

My wife instructed the maid to double-check all the doors and windows in the house and to make sure they were tightly closed. The next day Nabi repeated the same performance. My wife showed symptoms of nervous distress brought on by the crying of the cat. She entreated me to chase off Nabi. The cat must, by now, have realized that she had been expelled because of my wife's hatred. Whenever she sensed someone was around, she would melt into the darkness in the twinkling of an eye. There was, therefore, nothing that I could do to get rid of the cat.

To make matters worse, the cat never appeared for even a moment in the daytime. She showed up only at night, yowling. Upon being chased, she would disappear, and then reappear later and go on yowling. I could not figure out a way to get rid of her. In the end, I, too, had developed a loathing toward her. My wife implored me to kill the cat. Not being able to stand my wife's nagging any longer, I decided to honor her request and asked the maid to boil some water.

Carrying a large bowl of scalding water, I went upstairs and waited for the cat to show up and cry. I waited for the cat in darkness, holding my breath, until her two shiny eyes appeared, reminding me of a ghost. I waited until Nabi came closer to the window of our bedroom.

In a flash, as soon as I sensed Nabi's presence close to the wall, I poured boiling water down on her. I heard her short, pained cry of distress at the same time the hot water was streaking down the wall. I went outside to look for her, but I could find no trace.

After that night Nabi never reappeared again. She must have been horribly burned by the hot water! And where could she be now? Was she dead or alive? I wondered. I did not know for sure, but I had a strong feeling that she must have hidden herself somewhere in a dank, musty place and slowly died, grinding her teeth until the end.

Abruptly, as if under a spell, I threw the fruit knife. The knife hit the vinyl dresser, then fell on the floor with a dull metal sound. Once, a long time ago, I had seen the uncomprehending eyes of a cow. With the same eyes, I looked down at the knife. Slowly, I approached the knife and picked it up. Then I closely inspected the vinyl dresser. I saw that the spot where the knife had left its mark was slowly ripping open like a scar.

Momentarily, out of nervousness, I was tempted to fling the fruit knife away, but changed my mind and put it inside my pocket. Reason within me made me think I might need it again. Even if it did not function in its own capable way now, the knife might be reassuring just by its weight in my pocket.

I went out into the hall, grabbed the intercom on the wall and switched it on. For a moment, I gazed at the buttons on the wall downstairs flashing brightly and intermittently. At the same time, I tried to breathe steadily.

My thoughts wandered for a short while. I hesitated. Should I push the button for my wife's room or my mother-in-law's? Betraying my heart, I found my fingertip pushing the button to my mother-in-law's room. I heard the signal transmit a rasping sound, which must have been the intercom buzzing in her room. If I could have tolerated such a shrieking noise, I might have been able to be more patient with myself, hanging on to the intercom. I wanted to give them the impression that I was more at ease than they.

"It's me," my mother-in-law said. "Oh, is that you?"

"I'd like to see you," I said.

"Come to my room, please."

"Well, I prefer the living room."

"All right, then." She hung up first, slamming the receiver down sharply. Once again, I was wrapped in a sense of despair. She might be well-armored while I was unprepared to face her.

She might carry a solid shield that could not be penetrated even with a sharp-edged spear. Dejected, I thought of the fruit knife inside my pocket, the knife that failed to even cut through the vinyl dresser in my room. She might have already oiled that shield.

My mother-in-law was already lounging on the sofa, awaiting my arrival. I sat directly facing her. Today her face looked much larger. Like a certain reptile, which changes its body color depending on the environment it is in, she must have already changed her face in order to challenge me, I thought. Her eyes fixed on me. She looked at me with an air of contempt. You, you weak person, you have finally made up your mind — any condition you name will be of little or no importance, you detestable fellow — to me her expression conveyed these thoughts. She gazed at me arrogantly. Again, I was paralyzed with despair.

Suddenly, I heard the ebbing of a tide somewhere. On the other hand, it might have been the sound of a rising tide. I was not sure which. If it were incoming, though, such a tide quietly and slowly approaching land, it would not be making such loud and furious noises. Judging from the intensity of the sound, it must be an ebb tide running out into the sea, racing frantically like a gale as the moon wanes.

Once, a long time ago, I had been plagued by the sound of the ebb tide. On that particular night, I had not attended my night school class because I owed tuition for five months. Instead, I went out to the night sea where its sound raked through my heart. Now, I was experiencing the same sentiment within me, mistaking it for the sound of an ebb tide somewhere.

"I turned in my resignation today." I made this statement in confusion. I did not know how to begin the conversation. My mother-in-law watched me absently.

"Is there any way I can see my wife?" I asked. My mother-in-law's blackish lips looked abnormally thick.

"She isn't home now. It'll be a few months before you can see her."

I nearly shouted at her not to lie but bit my lip instead and only shuddered.

"I'd like to talk to her if I can." I managed to say after a brief interval.

"I understand she has said everything that needed to be said. If you see her again, it would be embarrassing for both of you. Do you understand that?"

I felt the weight of the fruit knife in my pocket at that moment. Why am I this weak and foolish? I accused myself. I realized I was not in a position to demand a meeting with my wife or even to demand an explanation.

"We tried everything we could possibly think of to change her mind. In spite of our efforts, she won't yield. You know how stubborn she is. Anyway, my husband and I have given up trying to persuade her."

I closed my eyes, momentarily blinded by the shining sunrays that were reflecting off my mother-in-law's oil-drenched shield. The only function the fruit knife could perform was to peel fruit. Ordinary human intelligence tells one that different knives are required under different circumstances.

"Well, anyway, how can we handle this matter? There's nothing that we can do. It's entirely up to you now. Take care of it as you think best," my mother-in-law said. As she was speaking, I found myself unconsciously nodding my head.

"I admit my daughter is a bad woman for behaving the way she is. But, I must respect her for having her own will, too. I'm afraid it's too late for you to try to change her mind."

At this remark, the doorknob I had previously seen flashed into my mind — the doorknob that sent out shiny silvery light in such a proud manner. My wife has already taken the key away from me — the key by which she could unlock her world by herself.

"In any event, I'd like to see her one more time and listen to her story with my own ears. For my own satisfaction, that is!"

"I hate to tell you this, but she made the remark that you're no better than a crippled person yourself because you married a cripple. She further stated that you're only suitable for a wife who is wholly deprived of the use of her legs. Beyond a shadow of a doubt, she believes that someone who can satisfy a normal, healthy person like herself must be waiting for her somewhere out there."

Not only had she prepared the shield, but my mother-in-law was also wielding a sharp-edged spear. A lump of ice formed itself in my heart. It took me a while to collect my wits. I was tempted to argue, "Once you tried to tempt me by telling me that I wouldn't be marrying your daughter; I would be marrying you and your husband. Now, are you trying to tell me that that promise was false and its time has expired?" Instead, I quietly put my hand into my pocket where I could feel the knife. Momentarily, my mind almost capitulated before I could come to my senses. I put my hand deeper into the pocket and felt my name seal. I took it out and placed it on the table, signifying my consent to a divorce.

My mother-in-law's eyes opened wider momentarily, and then her attitude became less severe. With great effort, I swallowed.

"Wait here just a minute, please," she said and then she went to her room. She brought out some papers placed them in front of me. They were papers necessary for the divorce procedure. All the entries had already been complete. Even my wife's seal was affixed by her name. Silently, I affixed my seal by my name on the document. I must have put too much strength on my seal. As a result, my name was imprinted deeply into the paper.

My hand was shaking. I hoped that the color of my face at that moment was not as crimson as the red ink pad. The energy of my entire body was going out through my legs and toes. Trying to compose myself, I barely managed to stand up. I chewed my lip. Now, there was nothing left for me to do in this house except to carry out the last step — I should walk out voluntarily.

Regardless of my will, I was not confident that I had enough strength left in my legs to walk out. Already standing, I forced myself to maintain that posture. At the slightest lessening of concentration, I would have opened my mouth to ask for a sip of water. I had to sweat it out and try to avoid such a tempting request.

Paying no attention to my legs' weak condition, my mind kept telling me that I must walk out just as I was. How long had I been debating? I looked at my mother-in-law. Again, I had to refrain myself from uttering the phrase, "A sip of water, please!" Slowly I turned my back to her. A small plastic trash can by the sofa caught my eyes. Abruptly the knife inside my pocket popped into my head. As I looked back at my mother-in-law, I took it out of my pocket. My fierce gaze met her bewildered eyes. As I saw her eyes become wider in surprise, I looked away. Then, I threw the fruit knife into the trash can.

"Take good care of yourself." I was finally able to say as I left the entrance hall of the house.

"Oh, dear, you're not going to leave like this, are you? Please wait a bit," my mother-in-law said imploringly, following me out into the hall. "My husband should be home at any minute. Please see him before you leave."

"Give my regards to him," I said.

"Don't leave this way, please. My husband has prepared something for you."

I shook my head emphatically.

"If and when I change my mind, I'll contact you," I said, thinking that I would go as far away as I could.

"Aren't you going to pack your personal belongings?"

"Please burn them for me." I said it easily before I could even think. "Throw them into an inferno that will consume the entire world." I muttered the last sentence to myself, taking big strides toward the front gate. How many steps did I take? Suddenly I thought of the wheelchair. My eyes ran to the side of the open shed. As I expected, it was still standing there by the wall of the shed, getting rustier each day.

The first time I had seen the wheelchair by the shed, I had

been very startled because it had been one of my wife's most valuable belongings. It was a mystery to me why they chose to leave it: by the shed where people could not miss seeing it as they came and went out of the house. It could have been stored inside the shed; if not in the shed, there was a storeroom by the kitchen, or it could have been put in the basement. The wheelchair had been sitting in the same spot till today, gradually rusting away.

Impulsively, my feet led me toward the wheelchair. Fiercely, I grabbed its handles and looked up at my mother-in-law briefly. She merely watched me in bewilderment. Clutching the wheelchair violently, I pulled it after me and opened the gate.

"I'll take this with me," I shouted.

"I urge you to see my husband before you leave. He has prepared something for you." My mother-in-law repeated the same plea again.

Not paying any attention to her, I pulled the wheelchair out of the front gate and I slammed the gate shut. This gate will never open for me again, I thought.

Pushing the wheelchair, I went out onto the main street, walking with much difficulty.

As I recall that time now, it makes me terribly ashamed. I cannot imagine what drove me to do such an embarrassing thing. I feel as if a couple of caterpillars are crawling down my back as I remember. I suppose I had no choice then but to act as I did since I was hysterically excited by the whole affair. By conducting myself as I did, I believed, I left a knife in the hearts of my wife and her parents. Besides that, I was overcome with shame.

There I was, on the one hand furious, on the other incapacitated with shame. I harbored an iron grudge against them. I walked away with a mincing gait, while people stared as I pushed the wheelchair in front of me down the middle of the sidewalk.

Translated by Hyun-jae Yee Sallee

THE TRAP

BUM-SHIN PARK

When I returned from my parents' house after being away almost eight months, my mother-in-law was squatting by the main gate. Only the posts remained, the door flaps having fallen off.

"Mother, I'm home," I said.

She flashed a glance at me. Although dusk was starting to gather around the thick vegetation of Mount Mae-bong, I could see that her face had aged completely in the eight months of my absence. Her white hair stood out like stiff wire, liver spots dotted her shriveled face and phlegm rumbled in her throat. The fierce gleam in her eyes made her appear inhuman. Amidst the death and destruction of the war, she had aged drastically, and I felt a surge of pity for the old lady.

"You've been having a hard time, haven't you? Where's Father?"

As soon as I had spoken, the old lady grasped my hand and waved her other hand as if to say, "Don't ask."

"It's time for your father-in-law to come," she whispered rapidly. I didn't know what the problem was, but I said nothing because of the old lady's expression and tense manner. The house was quiet. Weeds were growing between the roof tiles, and a portion of the roof had crumbled. But besides that, it basically did not look any different.

In spite of this, however, I detected an odor of death in the house as soon as I walked through the main gate. So it was. The whole building was like a stagnant swamp filled with some strange, chilly atmosphere. For no apparent reason, I shuddered, and the back of my neck trembled as I followed the old lady's gaze in the direction of Mount Mae-bong. The mountain gradually sloped up in back of the isolated house and from where Fan Rock jutted up shrubs grew and the slope rose steeply at an angle of thirty degrees. I noticed the old lady was staring at Fan Rock. Although the light of the setting sun still lingered on Mount Mae-bong, darkness had already settled on Fan Rock and only its form could be seen.

"Ruff! Ruff!" The old lady listened to the sound of a wolf or dog. "He's coming!" Trembling with fear, she grabbed my wrists with such force that I almost screamed.

"Who is it, Mother?"

"It's your father-in-law."

The source of the sound, which broke out intermittently, seemed to be coming closer. Rather than a bark, it sounded more like a death scream, conjuring up images of foaming at the mouth and the grinding of teeth.

Swallowing hard, I thought of the day I left the house. Father was standing at the main gate with Rusty at his side. The beast was a really beautiful shepherd. He was so huge that his paws were the size of puppies, and when he ran, he looked just like a wolf. About two months before this, my father-in-law had gone up to the mountain around dusk. There he had found this dog caught in a trap, his leg broken. He dragged him home.

"When war breaks out, animals suffer too. It would seem his

master couldn't take care of him, and the dog has been running around the mountains. If it wasn't for me, he'd have died by now," my father-in-law said. He named the dog Rusty because of his yellowish-brown color.

Rusty had apparently not eaten for several days, and his ribs were showing. However, for some reason he spent a whole day grinding his teeth and growling and would not come in to eat.

However, as soon as my husband threw him a piece of raw rabbit meat, the dog gobbled it up and licked his chops with a hungry look in his eyes. "Father, look how that dog loves raw meat!" my husband said. "When you call him, he runs away. You can try to grab him, but his muzzle is matted with blood. He's got a taste for blood so it's not going to be easy to tame him."

"If we try to tame him, he'll be even harder to handle. Let's see what happens if we just leave him alone. He won't last more than two days by himself," my father-in-law said.

My father-in-law's prediction was right. The dog did not last two days before he started eating rice. My father-in-law took great pains in healing the dog's paw. And before a month expired, you could untie his leash, and he would show no sign of wanting to leave.

"What did I tell you? You can tame an animal just like that!" my father-in-law said.

I could see that my father-in-law was satisfied, but my husband just would not give in. He would aimlessly kick the dog, muttering "He gives me the shivers." My husband was definitely engrossed in some ominous plot.

On the evening before we left to see my folks for a while, my father-in-law kept complaining, "You young people are a problem. What's going to happen to old folks like us?" My husband urged his father, above all else, to chase Rusty back to the woods.

"Don't worry. Even without you two in this isolated house, I'll be all right with Rusty." When it came to keeping Rusty around the house, my father-in-law's mind was set just as firmly as his son's.

"Well, I don't think so, Father. No matter what you say, that dog reeks blood."

In the end, my husband failed to convince his father. It seemed to me that in his state of anxiety, his power of persuasion had left him. However, even after we reached my parents' home, my husband was unable to forget his evil thoughts about Rusty.

"I'll go back home first," my husband finally suggested. The fact that my husband made that proposition a month ago was an indication of how strongly his mind had been disturbed by his deep-rooted hostility toward Rusty. I could not stop my husband. Although his idea might have been completely unreasonable, in the midst of a war, when you could easily see fly-covered corpses stuck on bamboo poles, how could I keep my husband from checking up on his parents?

"Look at that!" The old lady's explanation brought me back to the present moment. She rubbed her hands together nervously and panted, "That's your father-in-law, isn't it?"

In an instant I caught sight of the torso of a huge dog staring down at us haughtily from atop Fan Rock. The dog's bark reverberated into the many valleys surrounding Mount Mae-bong. At that moment, a dark figure suddenly sprang up like a wildcat on the edge of the rock and instantaneously the dog howled with even sharper animosity and dashed off into the darkness.

"That fool. . . what an idiot, his own father. . ." the old lady exclaimed. Then I realized the figure appearing for a moment on the edge of the rock before coming toward us was my husband.

Clacking her tongue, the old lady suddenly stood up and tottered off in the direction of Fan Rock. I was fixed to the spot like a stone statue and stood quivering as darkness seemed to descend upon me instantly. Although I could not tell exactly what it was, I felt that the seeds of some fateful plan, concealed in swamp-like obscurity, were beginning to ruin our household.

The monsoon rains came. It was really a dreary rainy season.

As June passed, the rain would fall each night and envelop Mount Mae-bong's twelve rugged peaks. It would run down the dreary faces of the rocks along the edge of the weeds and settle upon the rooftop of the old house. The rain would seep between the cracks of the broken roof tiles, eating away the clay underneath bit by bit and staining the ceiling, which was plastered with newspaper. The sogginess leaked along the door frame, the wall, the floor, and even into the bloodthirsty expression of the old lady who stared like a ghost with only that gleam in her eyes.

For a while, there were no changes in the household. The old lady practically confined herself to her room in darkness, and my husband went back and forth in the rain between the shed and Fan Rock as if he were planning something secretive. For a couple of days at first, I merely cleaned house and made an effort to break the tense atmosphere by talking to the old lady, but after a week I became lazy and did nothing but prepare meals. Maybe "lazy" is not the right word. No matter how much I chatted and managed to keep things swept as before, I became depressed by the morbid atmosphere of the house, by the old lady stubbornly hiding her feelings, and by my husband. Before several more days had passed, not only did I become increasingly depressed as if I were sinking down into a bottomless swamp, but I began to realize vaguely that the atmosphere of the house was slowly poisoning my consciousness, too.

"Would you tell me about Father?" I asked my husband, unable to restrain myself.

"He's dead," came the response that summed up the whole situation.

It did not seem as if the monsoon season would end soon. During the day, bright rays of sunlight would shine through the gray clouds, but at night, the rain would fall steadily without wind. The stream behind the house had risen conspicuously so that you could not even cross the stepping stones that led to the village without the risk of getting wet.

The old lady and my husband did not eat together. For each meal, I had to prepare two trays. When I carried the tray into the old lady's room, a rotten odor penetrated my nose.

"I'll have to open the door a bit, Mother."

"Don't bother."

Already the old lady was abnormal. From her weakening body, she coughed up a chamber pot full of phlegm and spent the day lying listlessly on the gloomy floormat. Even so, she ate a lot, and she handled her spoon and chopsticks with unrestrained gusto.

At suppertime, she always asked for more rice in a hoarse voice.

"What are you going to do with it?" I asked.

"I told you! It's to take to your father-in-law."

"But Father is dead."

"What!" The old lady's voice became shrill, and the look in her eyes changed right away. Her feeble pupils became steamed.

"Hell! You don't feed my man, your father-in-law? Well, that's not going to happen before I'm six feet under!"

Suddenly, in an instant, grinding her teeth, she collapsed like wet wallpaper. "Oh, please prepare one bowl of rice. Go get it without your husband's knowing. Think of it, if my husband comes so far in the rain and has to go back to the mountain without eating."

As she said this, she clung miserably to my skirt. If I gave her some rice, she would hide it in her skirt and, glancing furtively at her son's room, she would head for Fan Rock. Although washed by the rain every day, the flat surface of the rock became messy with the rice and side dishes that the old lady placed there.

"Hey, you tell your husband he's got to stop." The old lady would grumble, grabbing my wrist until it hurt and pointing to the shed where my husband was. "You have to stop him from whatever it is he's doing. It looks like he's gone out of his mind trying to kill Rusty, who's been possessed by your father-in-law's soul. Please, you've got to tell him to stop."

Truly, my husband spent every day in the shed making traps. He collected them from somewhere and would put together about three at a time. He carefully laid them, dripping with clumps of meat drenched with rabbit blood, in the vicinity of Fan Rock.

"I've got to catch that beast. If I don't catch him, he'll get Mother and all our family. That's no ordinary dog. He's possessed by an evil spirit," my husband said.

It seemed as though it was not the dog but my husband who was possessed by an evil spirit. As he went out carrying the traps, my husband's face was filled with hostility and murderous venom. Having sniffed blood, it seemed as if he would have no peace until the dog's carcass had rotted and the bones had turned to dust.

What on earth was happening? During the several months that my husband and mother-in-law were being destroyed, none of their friends seemed to wonder about the true nature of the plot which was slowly dragging our household into inexorable ruin. At first I felt suspicion, then despair, and finally a fascination for the obscure destructive forces surrounding me. I shut myself up in the old house in the midst of the decay-breeding monsoon. Everything was dying and decaying and slowly being eaten away.

Only the sound of rats cut through the uneasy silence as if to carve out their own place. When I heard the rats scratching beneath the floorboards and behind the cabinets, my hair stood on end. Once a rat as big as a kitten fell through a hole in the ceiling, and another time two or three new-born rats crawled from behind a pile of wood in the kitchen. In all the nooks and crannies of the house, rats were squeaking, dying and decaying, and being born. I was so nervous and exhausted that my lips became blistered. If only that beast could have caught these rats, things would have cleared up like a dense fog lifting.

I bought a gourd of potatoes and, balancing them on my head, crossed the stream up to my waist in cold water. Although it was dangerous, I had no choice but to cross over into the village in search of rat poison. At the entrance to the village was a store that displayed rubber shoes and white paper and even sold rice wine. Rat poison and ointments for emergencies were also sold there. Inside, though, it was empty. It seemed as if there were no goods or people. Disappointed, I was about to turn back when I noticed a pair of young eyes staring at me from a hole in the sliding lattice-door.

"You're Wang-gu, aren't you?" I asked.

Sliding the door, the ten-year-old son of the store owner slipped into a corner of the room and peered at me furtively. "What's the matter? Are you scared of me?" I asked. Wang-gu nodded his head. I realized that I would have to calm the child's fears first.

"Where did your mama go?"

". . . to get something."

"What?" I asked.

"Some food."

"Oh, my! You're out of supplies so you must be hungry. How'd you like a potato?" I untied my bundle. As soon as I took out some potatoes, the boy's mouth started to water.

"Even though they're raw, have some. It's okay. Come on, have some."

Hesitating for a second, he slid over on his knees and snatched a potato. I did not miss my opportunity.

"Got any rat poison?" I asked.

Taking the potato out of his mouth, he slid back into the corner.

"I mean there are just so many rats in our house. If you've got any rat poison, give me just one bag. You can have all these potatoes."

Wang-gu finally relaxed. It had not even taken me five minutes to bring him around. I took two packages of rat poison out of the box that he pushed over towards me and stuck them inside my jacket. Suddenly, with his mouth stuffed full of potatoes,

Wang-gu said something that made me spin around on my heels.

"You wanna kill the rats or the dog?"

"Dog? What dog?" I asked.

"You know what dog!"

"What. . . How could you think of such a thing?" I cried.

Realizing that the hair all over my body was standing on end, I asked the question in an effort to appear calm.

"That's what Mama says. The dog's a hundred-year-old fox, so it eats human flesh."

In an instant I sprung up. "Eats human flesh!" The spectre of that huge dog greedily devouring my father-in-law's flesh loomed large. That snarling beast was ripping off arms, legs, ribs, tearing out the kidney and the heart, and finally, like a fox at a baby's grave, digging out the eyes and eating them.

Before he was dragged to our house, the beast had acquired a taste for human flesh. He had lost his master during the upheavals and wandered around with nothing to eat. At a time when people were at the point of starvation, who would have taken care of a stray dog? Whether it was the soldiers or refugees, people's first thought would be to capture and eat him. So naturally the dog came to be afraid of people. Actually, you could say he became the enemy of humans. So instead of staying near starving people, the dog kept to the mountains and devoured pieces of flesh from corpses.

On that particular night, my husband explained the situation to me. According to him, four days after we left my parents' village, the People's Army came in. When the People's Army first gathered the villagers in the district manager's courtyard, the villagers realized that Young-phal was one of the soldiers who would be responsible for the villagers' fate. This was the first symptom of the cruel bloodbath.

Young-phal had a snub nose and a deformed arm. His left arm was withered and slightly bent so it would not flex. He had an unnatural gait and gave off a nauseating stench. My husband explained, "About five years ago when Young-phal was about fifteen, 'Buck Teeth,' his mother, used to appear in the neighborhood with her son Young-phal hanging onto her skirt. In our boredom we couldn't help throwing stones at them."

The mother and son, "Buck Teeth" and "Gimpy Arm," lived in their own peculiar way in back of the village in a shack where funeral equipment was kept. They helped around the neighborhood in order to get something to eat, and if there was not any work, they left for another village and sometimes were gone for a week. The mother and son were the laughing stock among the local kids. Young-phal was good at doing handstands. If the kids ran up throwing stones, he would smile broadly and, balancing with his bent and withered left arm, he would flip over on his right arm. Rocking back and forth in a handstand, he would balance the left arm, which looked about to break, with the right arm slightly bent. His eyes would glare, as if they might pop out, and his face would turn red.

At first the children kept their mouths shut in amazement; then they became afraid because of Young-phal's expression as he desperately held on. Then they would become riled with jealousy and reproachfulness at the sight of a cripple doing something they could not do, and they would start to throw stones at Young-phal while he was still doing his handstand. Even so, Young-phal did not straighten back up right away. Once, his forehead was covered with blood from a stone thrown by my husband. Young-phal was not able to straighten up for awhile.

At any rate, the year before the war broke out, Young-phal disappeared from our neighborhood because of his mother's death. It was my father-in-law who discovered Buck Teeth's almost rotten corpse when he passed in back of the funeral house. That was after Young-phal had already left the area. Five years later when Young-phal returned to the neighborhood, the first thing he did was to try to determine what had become of the kids who once threw stones at him. But this was not an easy task since they had grown up and either gone into the army or escaped.

Young-phal spent this time cruelly snooping from house to

house. At a certain point, Rusty, having put some flesh on his ribs, began to follow Young-phal around. Young-phal trained Rusty. First, he threw bloody rabbits to him and then trained him to hunt jack rabbits. When a rabbit would tremble with fear and hop backwards, trying to escape Rusty's mouth and front paws, Young-phal's narrow-eyed expression and Rusty's glare would be almost exactly alike. After several days without food, Rusty would howl terrifyingly and tear his prey into shreds taking revenge in a wild frenzy.

"With the battle winding down and retreat inevitable, that scoundrel Young-phal showed his true colors." As he spoke, my husband's forehead was like a sheet of white paper filling up with spots. "Ordinarily the people of the village would be captured and then left to die, impaled on bamboo poles. Without fail Rusty would search out those hiding in the mountains — even Father hiding behind Fan Rock. And yet. . .and yet . . ." My husband shuddered.

The next night, my mother-in-law sensed something horrible. She headed for Fan Rock and found out Rusty had gnawed up my father-in-law's corpse. Rusty must have been starving for days by the looks of my father-in-law's thigh, which had been ripped completely open.

The rainy season continued. Every evening the old lady put some food on Fan Rock, and my husband laid a trap. Rusty did not appear for a while. Days passed when it seemed as if something must happen, but we all did nothing. In the mornings, a stagnant atmosphere of hatred would surround the house. By evening, we would be wound in knots of bent tension, like bamboo poles tied with string. All three of us had our own plots, and we were waiting for Rusty to appear. But Rusty frustrated our hopes. Once we thought we could hear Rusty howling, but the night was too dark to make out his form.

After coming back from Fan Rock, my husband ground his teeth and said, "That animal keeps getting worse. He comes up without a sound, eats what he wants and runs off. Is there any rat poison left?"

"Rat poison? Why?" I asked.

"He only ate half the food that mother put there, so starting tomorrow, mix it with rat poison."

"I — I can't"

I could not do such a thing. Although I did not believe as my mother-in-law did that my father-in-law's spirit had gone into Rusty, I had no intention of assisting my husband in his scheme. It seemed to me that this was nothing but senseless killing. How on earth could anyone think that all misfortune was caused by one dog?

"You're seeing Young-phal's spirit in Rusty. Mother is the same," I cried disheartedly, pinpointing my husband's and the old lady's mistake. My husband was obsessed with revenge, while my mother-in-law's obsession was to remain as close as possible to the area of the killing and embellish Rusty's possession of her husband's spirit.

It seemed as if the situation was already at the point of no return, and I was seized with the uneasy feeling that in a short while it would reach a climax. Three more days passed when the old lady came back from Fan Rock trembling, and the drama swelled toward the conclusion.

"How in the world. . . how. . ." Even though the old lady was clutching the rice bowl she had brought back from Fan Rock and was screaming at my husband standing at the other side of the room, I did not catch on right away.

"Mixing rat poison in your father's rice bowl!"

"Father's dead." My husband's expression froze. At that moment, I realized that my husband had stolen the rat poison without my knowledge and put it in the rice bowl on Fan Rock, and I saw the old lady's terror.

"He's dead! It's Rusty who killed Father!" my husband shrieked.

"No," the old lady sputtered, "you're trying to kill Rusty, the reincarnation of your father!"

"I'm telling you that's not true!"

"It is true. Why don't you know your own father, who couldn't die peacefully because he had too much sorrow?"

"Rusty is an evil spirit."

"No, he is your father's reincarnation!"

"Mother, I'm telling you he is an evil spirit."

"I say no! You'll kill him. You'll certainly kill Rusty. You can't do that!"

"I'll do it. . .I'll. . ."

"You filthy murderer!"

The old lady lost control and wildly hurled the brass bowl containing the rice, colored purple by the poison. Fresh blood immediately appeared on my husband's forehead. At that moment, through a hole in the wall washed out by the rain, we heard Rusty howling close by. I groaned softly to myself. Right at the gate, which had rotted off, Rusty was standing and staring at us. Since it was already dark, we could not see him clearly. The two eyes seemed to emit blue phosphorescent light.

"That miserable dog!" I muttered.

At almost the same instant, my husband reached for a kitchen knife and the old lady grabbed his waist.

"Get out quick! The boy's gone mad!" The old lady struggled. "Calm down . . . please get hold of yourself. . .the bloodline. . .if you cut it off this way. Please get out! Get out! Get out!"

Leaving a trail like a snake skin in the wet earth of the yard, the old lady hung on to my husband's belt and was dragged along. Giving a howl, Rusty had already hidden from this madness behind Fan Rock.

The month of July slowly dragged to a close. As the gloomy monsoon gave way to August heat, we had our last storms. I slept fitfully because of the thunder and lightning, and every morning I started my day collecting the dead rats. Even if I did nothing else but mix up the rat poison, they kept on dying. They died in the corner of the soaked yard; they died on the terrace; they died under the cabinet or behind the wooden chest. They even died on the roof or under the floor. Once a day I made a pile of dead rats. I dug graves the size of a soup bowl and put a fist-sized stone on each. The old lady and my husband did not, or could not, understand the little graves. I lacked the killing instinct in my blood and this was a sign of my remorse.

Beginning in August, Rusty appeared almost every night at Fan Rock. In the evening, my husband would lay two or three or four traps and would spend most of his time near there. In contrast, the old lady's spirits dropped off sharply. No, actually this is not the right phrase. By that time, the old lady was so physically weak that she could not be nearly as active as my husband was. Her face became thinner as her spirits wilted, and when I would empty her chamber pot, there would be, unlike before, clots of blood. Even so, when my husband left, dragging the traps behind him, she would crawl on her knees to the door and remain there with her hands clasped, not budging until he returned.

"Tell him not to go," she would beg me as her eyes filled with tears. "Or both of you go far away. . . You don't believe that Rusty took over your father-in-law's spirit either? Huh, you can't believe it either?"

"Please calm down, Mother." I should have said out of pity that it was my husband who had gone out of his mind, but instead I snapped back at her: "Father is dead, killed by Rusty. Do you understand? We're in the middle of a war now."

The old lady's eyes filled with horror, "You're just as bad. . .not a bit of compassion!" She turned around and sat down. When my husband returned and I saw his pale, exhausted face, I thought that we would have to go someplace far away. But it was only a thought. One night would go by, and then I would face another night. The nights paralyzed me. Somehow the killing urge was seeping into me little by little. It was the waiting. If only the chilling conclusion could come quickly, if only the mad blood lust that penetrated the foundation of the decayed house would sweep through in an instant, then I would feel more settled. But when I finally encountered the fateful conclusion for which I had prepared all summer, contrary to my expectation, I felt only emptiness.

When the monsoon ended, Mae-bong peak appeared clearly with a fresh face for the first time. That night I heard Rusty howl. It was a more mournful cry than on earlier nights. I thought of waking my husband to check if Rusty was caught in a trap, but in the dark it would have been difficult. So I just closed my eyes again.

That was my mistake. In the morning when I saw the old lady's room empty, a sickening premonition warned me of what must have happened. I made a mad dash for Fan Rock. In the first bright morning sun of the summer, the horrifying conclusion sprang out at me. The old lady had been caught in a trap and had bled to death. Using her hands to pry herself free, she had left a trail of blood on the ground.

At first, I doubted that the old lady had the strength to free Rusty from the trap. After my husband buried the old lady and we left the village far behind, these doubts continued to torment me.

Translated by Dr. Teresa M. Hyun

ECHO, ECHO

—————————

JUNG-RAE CHO

"**U**ncle, I am going to get married."

My niece, In-hee, made this announcement calmly as she lifted her coffee cup. Startled, I was very close to saying, "Ah, you, already?" Thankfully, though, I swallowed the phrase; thus, I maintained my dignity as her uncle. The fact that my niece, In-hee, was now twenty-nine years old flashed through my mind as if it were some form of revelation. At the same time, I realized such an exclamation on my part would be unbecoming, considering her age. If I had made the remark, it might have demonstrated not only my usual irresponsibility, but also indifference towards my niece, who was raised without a father. My exclamation might have been suitable if In-hee had gotten married four or five years earlier, when she first reached marriageable age.

"Uncle, would you please go to the wedding hall with me and walk me down the aisle? Since my father hasn't returned yet. . . ."

Holding her coffee cup in both hands, In-hee spoke as quietly as before, her eyes on the cup. Unlike her, though, I was not poised, but felt goose pimples creeping all over my body at her remark.

"Yes, of course. Of course I will."

Trying to shake off this eerie sensation, I responded more loudly than necessary and squirmed in my seat, my eyes still fixed on In-hee. Her facial expression was as poised as her tone of voice.

"My father hasn't returned yet..." she had said quite matter of factly, as if her father wouldn't be able to make it home from an overseas trip in time for her wedding day. For the past twenty-nine years, since her birth, she had never seen her father's face. Considering this, I couldn't help being amazed at the way she was speaking of her father. Moreover, the calm expression on her face while she was speaking made me marvel at her even more.

In-hee's serenity was a carbon-copy of her mother's. My sister-in-law still seemed confident that her husband was alive. Her strong faith had been passed down without alteration to her daughter. No one had the heart to discourage In-hee's mother of her tireless, undying faith in the eventual return of her husband. Nor did anyone regard her attitude as being vain or hopeless, so I didn't utter a single word concerning my niece's manner.

Slowly I shifted my gaze from In-hee's face, which favored my older brother a great deal and yet carried a shadow of the melancholy of her mother. I found In-hee's extraordinary way of referring to her father truly eerie. Its similarity to her mother's attitude was responsible for my strange feeling. I experienced this same deeply somber mood whenever I saw the colorful, flapping garments of a shamaness. My sister-in-law took great pleasure in calling on such people.

"Even an educated person like you, In-hee?" I thought . . . Although disappointed in my niece, I realized that I too possessed the same illusion. The conviction my sister-in-law held regarding her husband's life was not the result of the omens of her favorite shamaness; rather, it was based on lack of proof to the contrary. During the war, notices of death were delivered as commonly as tax notices. In spite of this, official notice of my brother's death never reached our household. My sister-in-law's faith that her husband had survived was based on this fact. The shamaness' role was nothing more than a reinforcement of my sister-in-law's previously held conviction. In-hee, who was still confident that her father would return at any moment as if from a short trip, shared her mother's faith. How could anyone deny the evidence which had been implanted in their hearts?

Until my father's death, a certain family taboo existed in our household. No one was ever allowed to mention anything nega-tive or voice any doubt about my brother being alive. Even after my father's death, this taboo continued to be honored. Our household stubbornly refused to acknowledge the existence of the tall "Monument of the Unknown Soldiers," which continued to be customarily honored by representatives of any foreign countries visiting our National Cemetery.

"Well, I'd better be going." In-hee got up from the sofa.

"Oh, no. Don't go." I said, gesturing with my hand. I had not intended to say "don't" nor did I understand why I said it. "By the way, what kind of person is your groom-to-be?"

I managed to ask this question after sorting out some of my thoughts.

"We were going to come and see you together today, but this time of day was not suitable for him. We will come to see you in two or three days. Take care of yourself."

In-hee left my office briskly, giving me a stiff smile that strongly resembled her mother's. I looked blankly at the sofa where In-hee had been sitting.

I felt sorry for my niece. More than ever, I was engulfed in for-lorn hopelessness concerning my brother's return. In my niece's sad face, I saw the face of my brother and my father's face mir-rored side by side.

My brother and I were nine years apart in age. When my brother went to Japan to study to become a public prosecutor and judge, I was in the fourth grade.

"I'll give you generous financial support. You only concentrate on your studies and become an honorable prosecutor and judge. If you do, my son, your father will be as content as if he had gained everything possible under heaven." This was the statement my father made repeatedly to my brother. As to my father's vow of financial support at any length for my brother's education, we were indeed rich enough for him to keep it. Except for the fabric stores owned by the Japanese, my father's fabric shop was the largest in our town of Sa-ri-won. Along with his shop, he also had many acres of rice fields. My father kept his store at an operable size and continued to buy more rice fields with profit that he made from the store.

When my mother lost an occasional customer due to the limited assortment of goods in stock, she would become fretful and urge my father to expand the store a little. Whenever she would fuss and fume, my father would shut the door on her, ignoring the proposal.

"You thick-headed wife," he would storm, "don't you realize that losing customers to someone else hurts me, too? Do you think I'm not expanding the store because I don't know how? Expanding the store until it is bigger than the stores of the Japanese would be far easier than swallowing cold rice wrapped in lettuce. But, you must understand how the world is these days, my dear wife. Think. Where is the world heading? We'll be secure with second place in this business. In the meantime, we'll expand our land holdings wider and wider. The world may change unpredictably, but it is a rule that land is the one constant thing in this world."

After they had completed elementary school, my two older sisters stayed home, doing all the housework. They always grumbled about the work when my mother wasn't listening. Often, they would hurl the gourd water-dipper across the room in anger. They were unhappy about not being able to go to middle or high school in spite of the fact that we were wealthy.

"Girls don't need to learn anything else once they have mastered the Korean alphabet," our father told them. "Girls become ill-fated if they are educated, so learn everything about housekeeping and prepare yourselves for marriage."

At my father's words, my sisters knew there was no escape and that they must plunge themselves into housework.

It was one May morning when we received news from the police station that my brother had been arrested for taking part in the independence movement.

"Oh, what am I going to do now? Our family is ruined now! It's ruined! What am I going to do?" My father burst out, wailing louder than the lowing of an ox, pounding on the store's wooden floor with his hand. My father couldn't go on wailing for long, though, as he had to accompany the suspicious, sharp Japanese detective back to the station for questioning. The detective had come, not to deliver the news of my brother's arrest, but to arrest my father on account of my brother's crime.

At the thought that my father might be beaten, I was paralyzed. My heart palpitated when I thought of my brother who had taken part in the independence movement. I felt very confused.

During the long winter vacation before my brother left for Japan in March, he had done nothing but read books. He looked so handsome when he left, wearing a square college cap. During his first year-long stay in Japan, my brother was transformed into an adult just like my father. Moreover, my brother had become more taciturn than ever before. I found myself having more difficulty addressing my brother than even my father.

When he went to Japan again for his sophomore year in college, I saw him off with envy in my eyes. I had never pictured him as becoming active in the independence movement. Then as if to fulfill my heroic image of my brother, news reached us of his arrest while actively participating in the movement. I trembled with awe. After that, my father was summoned to the police station three or four more times.

"What a fool my son is, behaving in such an imprudent way, not caring what's really happening in the world! How could he act so carelessly! What an ungrateful son he is! He doesn't understand how his father feels."

My father took to frequent bouts of drinking. This was not like him. When he was drunk, he railed endlessly at my brother. My mother sighed deeply as she endured my father's drunken tirades.

"Don't say anything, wife. I didn't work this hard just to support a wretch like my son. He deserves to have a rough time in jail to teach him never to do such crazy things again."

My father would always shout like this at my mother, glaring fiercely at her. Finally my mother would become diffident and would only wipe her tears away, shrinking in my father's presence.

One harsh, windy day in December, my brother was released from prison and came home. When he came into our courtyard with my mother, who had gone to meet him at the train station, my father yelled a command at him.

"You miserable wretch, don't you dare come into the room. Just stay there where you are."

"Husband, why are you doing this to him? Why?" My mother cried quickly, seized with fear.

"Wife, you'd better stay out of this."

My father, stepping from the wooden porch, picked up a long rod from beside a pole where it had rested for a long time.

"You miserable boy, it would have been better if you had been killed after you joined that so-called 'independence movement.'" My father began to yell at my brother in a frenzy, while whipping his back with the rod. "Why are you creeping into my house now? You thick-headed, stupid fool! You had no business getting involved in such a mess. How dare you do such a thing when you're so ignorant of the situation in the world? How dare you? The great Japanese Empire is a tiger compared to you, standing as less than a mouse in front of it. How could you dare oppose it?

You idiot. You're not my son. Get out of this house! Go somewhere and die!"

My brother endured the lashes silently, tightly shutting his eyes.

"You'd better kill me. Kill me instead!" my mother cried. Unable to watch the whipping any longer, she threw herself between my father and my brother protecting my brother from further blows. My father's arm, holding the rod lifted high in the air, trembled violently before the harsh wind of his anger.

"You stupid fool." He continued to rant at my brother. "You carried a sheaf of straw on your back and then threw yourself into the fire!"

My father hurled the rod on the ground and stomped out of the house, kicking open the front gate. He returned home that night and drank himself unconscious.

For several days, my brother slept all day long. The whole house was permeated with the strong odor of Chinese herbs being boiled into medicine for him. After drinking the medicine, he lingered in sleep.

"What kind of beatings he must have received from Japanese police," my mother mumbled, fanning herself. "Otherwise, how could a young body like his have suffered so?"

She neglected the store entirely and devoted herself to tending the pot of Chinese herbs for my brother. I didn't need to ask my mother to confirm that my brother's weakness had nothing to do with the whipping he received from my father. It wasn't difficult to figure out that his weakness was caused by the brutality of the Japanese police.

I sat by my mother and waited to carry the bowl of medicine to my brother. While drinking the medicine, he never once looked at me, much less spoke. I studied his face closely while I waited until I could leave his room with the empty bowl.

Five days passed before my brother appeared to be regaining his health. I saw him sitting up, leaning against the wall. At times, an open book was laid on the floor by the head of his bed.

Finally, one day, my brother spoke to me as he took the medicine bowl from my hands. "You're going to a lot of trouble on my account."

I took advantage of this opportunity. I sat by him so close that my knees touched his and waited for him to finish drinking his medicine. He wiped his mouth with his palm and put the empty bowl on the floor.

"My brother," I started. I was taken aback by the sound of my own voice. It was strangely loud. I felt my face flush hotly. Instead of responding, my brother only regarded me questioningly.

"Uh, uh . . ." I began.

"Go ahead. You're free to say anything that's on your mind since we're alone." My brother stroked my hair, smiling. His gentle voice, his soft smile, and the unexpected warm touch of his hand, this impression of him is one of the clearest and most pleasant pictures of my brother that remains in my memory today.

"Uh, well, have you really taken part in the activities of the independence movement? How does it work, my brother?"

Somewhat encouraged, I quickly whispered these questions. For a good while my brother looked straight into my eyes. His own were shining more brilliantly than the noontide sun in summertime.

"I had to do it because of those Japanese bastards."

Lowering his head, my brother spoke. His voice was so faint that I could hardly hear him. His head shook from side to side. "I didn't achieve what I wanted to. I'm ashamed of myself, facing you like this," my brother said sadly, as if he were in mourning, gazing absent-mindedly at the ceiling. Then he was again looking into my eyes, but suddenly his countenance had become forbidding, and he was convulsed with rage. "Sang-kyu, you'll understand all this when you grow up a little bit more. Why don't you go outside and play?"

As if ejected by some force, I flew from his room. Sudden

dizziness overtook me. The wooden floor seemed to be wavering in front to my eyes. I couldn't comprehend what my brother was trying to tell me. At the same time, I felt such a sense of distance between my brother and me that he seemed a total stranger.

I was close to my graduation from the university before I finally began to understand what my brother meant when he spoke to me of "shame."

The Japanese police would not leave my brother alone. They began to pressure him to volunteer for the war as a student soldier.

"My husband, what have you saved money for? Your son's life hangs in the balance in this life and death situation." Thus, my mother entreated my father, her voice intense with emotion but he wouldn't listen to her heart-rending pleas.

"Don't be ridiculous!" he snarled. "He brought this on himself. We must marry off our daughters quickly in order to avoid further complications that might befall our family. That is our problem. Whether our son joins the army as a student is his problem."

My mother, who was tired of trying to reason with my father, now turned her pleading upon my brother.

"Sang-sup, my son, run away from this place. You can go either to Manchuria or deep into the mountains. I've heard that once a student is taken to the battlefield, he never returns." She seemed to be in agony as she pleaded with my brother.

"Mother, please try to understand," my brother said calmly, even smiling a little. "Fleeing won't solve anything. You don't need to worry about me. I'll handle this matter the best I know how."

But my brother had no alternative plan when he made this statement to my mother in this confident manner. Of his own volition, he went to the police station and signed a document volunteering for the war as a student. Compared to my mother's simplistic solution of running away, my brother's decision to join the army perhaps was best given the circumstances.

My mother, who only found out about my brother's decision later, stood with her legs planted far apart, defiantly facing my father.

"You have sent your son into the jaws of death because you are so stingy with your money," she accused. "You can't be human!"

"That mouth of yours! You'd better shut it before I beat you to death." My father flared at her, raising his clenched fist as if he were really going to strike my mother. My father often said that he was an ignorant man, but I had never in my life felt that he could be violent, too. He now seemed to be an ignorant, uncouth animal to me. There was no way my mother could physically match my father.

My mother had now come to the realization that my brother was going to war. The very next day she undertook a very difficult task. She selected the best silk in her store and then wrote on the fabric in Chinese characters the words "Your Success in War." Going frantically from house to house, she asked each person to make a single stitch on those four words until one thousand stitches from one thousand people were completed. If my brother carried on his body an object bearing this inscription, especially one made through the devotion of one thousand people, she believed that he could survive even in the face of death. While she devoted herself to this task, tears never left her eyes. Frequently, she even forgot to eat.

My mother was in torment, putting that inscribed piece of silk deep into my brother's pocket with care on the morning of his departure. "Don't part with this, not even for a second. Don't forget that, do you understand?"

My father said to him, "Try to avoid flying bullets. Then you'll be all right."

This remark was a classic example of his incredible ignorance. How could my brother possibly avoid flying bullets, which travel several hundred times faster than the speed at which a human can move? Even I, only in grade school, knew such things, while my father, an adult, did not. I hadn't realized that my father was that ignorant. The very thought of my father talking so loud and in such a crude manner made me shudder. I felt as if I wanted to die right then. However, my father never seemed to be ashamed of being so hopelessly ignorant.

In spite of his astounding ignorance, my father was gifted with the art of making money. Moreover, he knew how to calculate in his head without the aid of an abacus. It was uncanny how fast he could count.

Having been married off quickly in order to avoid the ignoble fate for which the Japanese Empire drafted single Korean women, my oldest sister now gave birth to a son. When yet another year had passed after his birth, we still had received no word from my brother. Every household was forced to give all kinds of brassware to the Japanese government. The authorities even took the railing from iron bridges.

"I don't understand it at all," my father muttered when he first heard the news that Korea was liberated from Japanese rule. "How strange and hard to believe, this sudden fall of Japan."

He cocked his head first to one side and then the other as if he were truly sorry that the Japanese Empire had fallen. He did not appear to be happy at all over Korea's liberation, although he could now expand his store without his success being investigated by Japanese merchants. In my father's eyes, this commercial advantage was of little concern.

"First of all, my husband, let's enlarge our store," was my mother's second remark after the news of Korea's liberation had exhilarated her so that she almost danced. The first thing she said was, of course, "My son, Sang-sup, can come home now!" Her voice choked with emotion.

"You wretched biddy," my father shouted at my mother. At that, my mother shut her mouth, truly looking like a dispirited little hen as my father yelled at her.

"This unsettled world . . .this wretched world. . . "

My father looked thoughtfully out the store windows, inhaling nervously on his cigarette. His expression was serious, as if he were concentrating on something gravely important.

Strange rumors began to spread through the town after the Russian Army took North Korea. According to the rumors, everyone, whether rich or poor, would live in equality; the world no longer would have discrimination. They said the Russian Army would make sure such a world came to the people. Whether or not he paid any attention to such rumors, my father began to make frequent visits to Pyongyang (the largest city in North Korea). His visits to Pyongyang did not result in his bringing home goods for the store. Shortly after this, in October, 1945, my brother returned home safely and in good health.

"You've been through hard times, my son," was the only remark my father made to my brother when he returned home from the war.

For three days and nights my brother ate and slept. This time he would not take any brewed Chinese herbs as he had done when he had returned home from jail for his role in the independence movement. My mother became impatient with him because of his stubborn refusal to take the medicine, which would strengthen his weakened body.

As soon as my brother's sleeping period was over, I asked him about a rare story which had been upsetting me terribly for quite some time.

"My brother, is it true that starving Japanese soldiers ate human flesh while fighting in Burma?"

My brother looked at me absent-mindedly for a short time and then asked bluntly, "Why? Would you like to taste human flesh, too?"

I was stunned at his abrupt question. A horrible picture flashed through my mind, a picture of a human with legs and arms cut off, the stomach ruptured. As I imagined such disgusting things, I became nauseated and started to vomit. I threw up my breakfast. Then, I shed bitter tears. I had never felt such hatred toward him before, nor such a distance between us.

My brother, dressed in his best, started going in and out of the house in a busy manner every day. He seemed to be noticeably animated and in high spirits. It was after only a few days that another battle erupted in our household.

"Sang-sup, you miserable son," my father rushed into the courtyard shouting. "I heard that you're the leader of the scouting party that arrests their own fathers. You death-deserving scum, you'd better come out of your room right now! I'll break both your legs with no mercy if you spend your time on such things after eating well at my table!"

My father was much more indignant than he had been at the time of the incident concerning the independence movement. He was holding a club in his hand this time, not just a stick. However, my brother wasn't about to be clubbed, nor suffer silently as before. He succeeded in taking the club away from my father while avoiding all his blows.

"Wait a minute! Have you gone mad? Are you ready to die now? How dare you attack your own father?" my father yelled, pounding on his own chest after the club had been taken away from him.

"Your beatings won't stop me from what I'm doing. It must be done at any cost to build for the future," my brother said in his usual dignified manner. The undertaking he was referring to was the Communist movement.

"Before God, you're absolutely ruining our family!" As if drained of energy, my father plopped down on the edge of the wooden porch, resting his head on his knees.

"I must have been a mad man, I should have taught you the art of business right after you attended grade school. I must have been out of my mind, hoping that you would become a prosecutor and judge. I supported you with money, money like chunks of gold, in order for you to be a prosecutor and judge who would bring prestige to our family. Instead, you are learning about Communism, which will surely destroy us. You fool! Have you lost your senses? Don't you know how we earned our fortune?

How dare you behave so insensibly? For four generations — your great-great grandfather, great grandfather, grandfather, and myself — we have pinched every penny in order for us to have this money that we have today. From generation to generation, you mindless ingrate, we have carried sacks on our backs regardless of the weather until our shoulders went numb. Snow or rain, hot or cold, our ancestors opened avenues for us to build a foundation for ourselves by peddling from village to village, crossing rivers and climbing mountains."

"Your grandfather, in particular, was a hard-working man. He was responsible for leaving me sufficient funds to open my present business. Do you have any idea what kind of hardships I've been through in order to build this fortune from my inheritance? Can you comprehend what made me determined to make you a prosecutor and judge regardless of the expense of your education? In spite of my good intentions, you have become a leader of the scouts who not only would destroy their fathers, but also the integrity of their entire families. Go ahead, you miserable son. You deserve to suffer a painful death, yes, you do!"

After he had delivered this stormy speech to my brother, my father yelled for someone to bring him a bowl of cold water. Like a post, my brother continued to stand in the center of the courtyard in the gathering dusk.

For a few months, until all of our property was confiscated, there were terrible scenes nearly every day. The reason for their endless quarreling was that my father kept pestering my brother to give up the ideology of Communism, while my brother stood by his convictions. Taking after my father in stubbornness, my brother persisted in confronting him. This was quite overwhelming to me.

My father seemed to lose his appetite for life after he had his property confiscated, although, through my brother's efforts, we were able to keep the house. We were fortunate compared to others. Other rich families or landlords had their previous servants come live in the main living quarters while they suffered the humiliation of having to live in a separate room that had formerly been for guests. In more grievous instances, people were dragged away and charged with being "pro-Japanese" or "reactionary."

Suddenly one day at the meal table, my father said, "Despite everything that is happening, I'll try to live through this Communist era. After all, it is only made of people, isn't it?"

He sounded as if he had learned to accept the fact that he could not afford to feel constantly frustrated any longer. His simple declaration lightened the hearts of every member of our family as if it were a sparkling flame in the darkness.

In the meantime, misfortune befell our family again. My brother was arrested by the public security police. He had thrown an ashtray at another person's head over an argument during a conference. The man was severely injured as a result.

My father heaved a long sigh after hearing about the incident. "You stupid fool, once you decided to become a Communist, you should have learned to keep your mouth shut even if you're unhappy about something. Why do you act so carelessly? You're an idiot, a stupid idiot!"

The fact that my brother injured the other person was not important. It was what my brother said that prompted his arrest. If it was proved that he spoke with an "anti-reactionary voice," he would have no guarantee of any kind of future whatsoever.

Five days after his arrest, my brother had not been released. More time elapsed. Instead of my brother coming home, a security policeman rushed unexpectedly into our house one day. After his visit, we lost our house.

Until my brother was released, we suffered severe hardships. We lived in a shack for a whole year. To obtain a food-allocation coupon from the authorities, my parents and my one remaining sister had to do hard labor in a work camp. And yet, we were always hungry. We lived on, not complaining of our hardships, with the hope that my brother would return home safely. In fact, no one in our family regarded our hard times as unbearable.

When he finally came home, my brother was unrecognizably thin after serving his term in prison.

"Sang-sup, do you still feel the same about the Communists?" my father asked in a low voice.

"Well. . ." My brother hung his head.

"I'm not blaming you, my son. Tell me the truth about how you feel. Please don't hide anything from me."

"I now agree with your sentiment about Communism, Father," he said, still hanging his head.

Abruptly, my father grasped my brother's hand. "Good. Let's leave for the South," he said unexpectedly.

Everyone's eyes instantly went toward the door. The room was as still as if everything were frozen.

"Yes, Father, let's do that," my brother finally responded. "When should we leave?" That was the first and last time my brother and father agreed on something so readily.

"About this time tomorrow night."

"I'm for your plan to leave immediately, but, Father, we're not ready yet."

"Leave everything to me."

We spent the next day in our usual routine except that my father excused himself from work, claiming to be sick. He went to some mysterious place that day. After an early supper, we left the house after darkness fell.

Two full nights we walked; our destination the town of Haeju. Three days after we left home, we arrived at Inchon by boat. My father paid the boatman, not with money, but with a piece of gold taken out of his belt.

"Because of concentrated patrol, it is dangerous to cross the 38th parallel on foot. Besides, I don't trust the guides. According to rumors, people have been swindled by these guides and some have even lost their lives," my father said, enjoying the rice and beef soup, his appetite being so hearty.

It was in a room at an inn in Seoul that we saw all the gold in the money bag that my father unfastened from his waist and laid on the floor.

"Don't let us lose heart just because this is a foreign city to us. Let us be strengthened by these nuggets and try to start life courageously again here," my father said in high spirits, holding thumb-sized pieces of gold in his hand.

"By the way," my mother asked, looking at my father with a contented smile, "how did you manage to get all that gold?"

Surprised by the fact that even my mother wasn't aware of my father's amazing gold, the rest of us just stared at our father.

"My wife, do you recall when you used to complain that I might have a mistress in Pyongyang because I made such frequent trips there? Well, that was when I purchased this gold."

"You're remarkable, indeed, my husband. How did you know the situation would come to this?"

"Please, my wife, say no more. If I were less ignorant, my precious property wouldn't have been confiscated so unfairly. I could have saved more than half of it. In such ignorance as mine though, I have been living in darkness, not knowing anything whatsoever about the existence of Communism in this world. I took action only after the Russian Army took over the North. That's the reason I managed to obtain only this much gold."

"Don't talk like that. How fortunate that we are able to save so much, my husband!"

While my mother was fingering the gold, my brother was sitting quietly, his head deeply bowed.

With proceeds from the sale of gold, we bought a small house outside of the East Gate. For nearly ten days my father went diligently about the city, and finally asked all of us to gather around him.

"I have decided to open a fabric shop again. As long as you can invest, you can make money easily here. People can earn a living by working hard in the South. This is a place where people can live well. The only livelihood I know is running a fabric shop. I'll start it all over again. Let's try to forget the past and go on living. Sang-sup, my son, why don't you come to work with me?"

I thought I had misunderstood my father's last words, but I hadn't. Suddenly my father shouted at my brother, whose head was lowered, "Why don't you answer me?"

"Well, I'd like to finish my interrupted education," my brother responded uncertainly.

"What? Study?" My father snorted as if my brother's statement was beyond him. He put a cigarette in his mouth.

"Please listen to me. We don't need an honorable prosecutor and judge in our family any longer. As you can see, we have been driven to a foreign city, and we must try to make a living here. We are facing a very trying time just to solve our imminent food problem. How can you find it in your heart to talk about continuing your education? We need to make a substantial amount of money first. After that you can expect your son to be a prosecutor and a judge."

"I realize that, Father, but . . ."

"Then why don't you stop talking nonsense? It's useless. If you feel you really need to continue your studies, you may try to support yourself. But you're not the only child I have to think about. I won't offer to help you."

My brother did not work for my father in his fabric shop, but he did not go back to school either. He did nothing for two months until, through the recommendation of an old schoolmate, he found himself a job elsewhere. My father, who was tied up in his new business, did not pay any attention to my brother's new job. However, my brother's job did not last long. An anonymous tip led to my brother's arrest on a charge of having once been a Communist.

"What a short-sighted fellow he is!" my father mumbled weakly after he had met with my brother in jail. "He should have realized when he joined the Communist Party that something like this would happen to him once he had followed the wrong crowd."

The police had a detailed record of my brother's activities in North Korea. But the fact that he served a prison term in the

North, was, of all things, completely missing from that record. My father said someone who came south from Sa-ri-won, our hometown, right before my brother's arrest, might have informed the authorities. In the view of the police, my brother was a true Communist who disguised himself and came south.

"Who could that unkind person be?" my mother asked worriedly, rubbing her palms together.

"How am I supposed to know? As you well know, Sa-ri-won is a large town where there were several wealthy families. Sang-sup must have made a lot of enemies among them. Most of those rich families, I'm sure, came south, whatever the cost. So you see, it should not be difficult for Sang-sup to understand how his arrest came about."

My father continuously smoked his cigarettes. He said that the verdict of innocence or guilty for my brother depended on the verification of his jail sentence in the North. Unfortunately, the line between the North and South was already set at the 38th parallel. No one was available from the North to testify about my brother's prison term except our own family members, and our word was not accepted by the authorities. As a result, my brother was sentenced to one more year in prison.

"I have no doubt in my mind that he was born under an unlucky star," my mother said tearfully. My father made a gutteral sound as if he were about to spit.

During my brother's imprisonment, my father threw himself into his business. Not even once did he go to see my brother. My mother did not blame my father for such behavior at all. It was as if she were grateful that he gave her his tacit consent for her to see her son in his cell.

My brother was completely worn out when he came home after serving his jail term. He confined himself in his room every day; when he did come out, he would stand gazing at the distant horizon. A few months after he came home, the Korean War broke out. It was my brother who began to seek refuge for us somewhere.

"According to radio news, we are safe here," my father said angrily. "Why don't we wait and see what's going to happen? Our side is not helpless, you know. Good grief! Why are they stirring this up, when my business was about to boom?"

While we were undecided on what to do, the North Korean Army invaded Seoul. According to widespread rumors, the Han River bridge had been destroyed. Our family went out to a near-by island on the river called Duk Island, but even the wealthiest person in town had no power to rent a boat. The river bank, where not a single boat was available, was teeming with refugees.

"Let's go back," Father said.

"No way," my brother insisted firmly.

"What do you mean, 'no'?"

"I'll cross the river."

"How can you?"

"I'll swim."

"You'll drown."

"I can make it."

"Are you sure?"

"Yes, I'm confident that I can."

"All right, then you go alone."

My father gave my brother a sum of money. His decision to leave Seoul turned out to be the best decision he had made in his lifetime. If he had stayed behind in Seoul, he would have been dragged into the war as a volunteer trooper, or he might have gone through harassment as a person who had illegally crossed over the 38th parallel into South Korea.

For four months, until my brother came back to us, I dreamed nearly every night that he was drowning in a very blue river. I couldn't share my dream with anyone, not even my sister.

"Someone very kind-hearted in Choong-chung Province saved my life," was the only statement my brother made to us when he returned, although we were anxious to find out how he had managed to survive in the midst of the whirlpool of war.

People said there had never been such a severe winter as that one. Due to a general retreat on January 4, 1951, Seoul became an empty city. Lines of refugees, walking through snowstorms and winds of gale force, headed for more southern parts of Korea. We, too, were a part of that mass of fleeing refugees. My brother wasn't with us, though. He joined the Second People's Army which was composed of desperate youth who were left behind.

We went down as far south as Nonsan City and stayed a while there. Then, following the National Army drive against the North Korean Army, we also returned to Seoul. As we walked into our home, we were greeted by a startling sight. My brother was already there awaiting us. There was also an unfamiliar woman with him.

"This is the person who saved my life, twice." My brother immediately presented her to my parents with these words. His introduction had a deep affect on us. Our suspicion was transformed into gratitude.

"I know there were big problems with the Army," he told us. "I can't tell you how bad it was. It was cold. The food supplied to the soldiers was very poor, too. As soldiers increased in number, discipline disintegrated. There were deserters then, and they plundered the others, unable to control their hunger pains. Some froze to death and some starved to death. It was a horrible experience. If I stayed, I knew I would end up like the dead soldiers. With that thought in mind, I ran away from my company and went back to see her again with no sense of shame."

"Those in charge of the troops and their food deserve to receive the rage of God ten times," my father ranted. "After they forced our precious young men to join the army in the name of an offensive drive north, they let these men starve and freeze to death. At the same time, a few high ranking officials practiced unforgivable corruption by taking money that was intended for food and clothing for the soldiers. They deserve death and posthumous beheading! With that kind of attitude, they won't be able to win the war. I tell you this country is rotten! Yes, rotten to the core."

My father did not hesitate to use abusive language even in the presence of a woman he had just met for the first time. My father was referring to the shameful treatment of soldiers in the Second People's Army during the war.

"I must get married," my brother said as decisively as he had spoken when he expressed his decision to swim across the Han River.

My parents merely looked at my brother for a while as if they were struck dumb. The woman sat with her head down.

"Judging from your good deed of saving my son's life twice, your marriage, no doubt, must be preordained by Providence, but. . ." Time seemed to crawl while my father rolled a cigarette with a piece of newspaper. "But since the war is still going on, why don't you wait and talk about it after the war is over?"

"No. No way," my brother barked abruptly. The woman, who had been sitting with her head lowered, was startled and changed her position. I was certain that no one in the room could possibly fail to be aware of my father grinding his teeth in disgust.

"Sang-sup," said my mother, "marriage is the happiest event in one's life. In the midst of war, how can you get married without anything being prepared?"

"Mother, we don't mind not having anything at all. Do you recall, in the olden days, marriage was performed with only a bowl of cold water on the table?"

Why in the world was my brother in such a hurry, I wondered. I couldn't understand his reasoning. He kept interrupting my parents before either of them could finish a complete sentence.

"Why don't you become engaged for now and go back to the countryside and stay until the war is over? I believe you should not get married until that time."

"Please, Mother, our circumstances do not permit that."

My brother raised his voice. My mother's expression showed that she had read some hidden message.

"All right, then, I understand. You can go ahead and get married."

My mother's quick agreement amazed me. It was the first time she had ever made a significant decision all by herself without consulting my father. My father was, in the meantime, staring at the floor silently, inhaling cigarette smoke.

The next day, as my mother promised, my brother got married over a small table covered with a white cloth. On it was placed a bowl of cold water. The wedding ceremony gave me the impression that they were merely playing a game. At the same time, watching such a ceremony, I felt a pang of sadness. The gravity that prevailed weighed heavily on my mind. Later when I became older, I learned that it was my sister-in-law's pregnancy that brought on this hurried wedding.

The war was still going on, though. My brother received a draft notice from the Army.

"Flee to your in-laws," my father said with no reservation whatsoever.

"No, Father, I don't want to."

"Escape, my son, or you'll face a senseless death."

"I don't think I want to run away, Father."

"Please listen to your dad for once in your life."

"I'll think it over."

My brother would not honor my father's suggestion in spite of his pleas. Four months after his wedding, my brother returned to the battlefield.

In the midst of uneasy times when unexpected notices of death-in-action came to nearly every household, my sister-in-law gave birth. The entire summer went by before the end of the war came. After the cease-fire, however, my brother did not return. Even after the exchange of the prisoners-of-war between the North and South, my brother did not come home. No one in our family, however, opened his mouth to say anything about whether he was alive or dead.

After the war, my father's business began to prosper rapidly.

He had to stay up nearly every night until midnight to count the money, which he then carelessly put into an American military duffle bag. After counting one hundred bills, he would wrap the bundle with a paper strip. My parents did not appear enthusiastic about counting the money, though. It was the same with my sister-in-law who helped my parents with counting and wrapping the money.

As she grew older, my niece, In-hee, became the exact image of my brother. Lost in thought, my father would gaze at his granddaughter, looking up in surprise whenever he noticed anyone else around.

My sister-in-law started to help my father in his store when her daughter entered the first grade. I did not know how it started, whether it was my father's idea or my sister-in-law's. Nevertheless, we were astonished to discover a new characteristic of my sister-in-law when she went to work for my father.

No one had suspected that a quiet, gentle, meek person like my sister-in-law would have the ability to do well in the rough world of business, but she proved all of us wrong. It turned out that she had a real head for business. I have often heard people say that the depths of another's heart is usually hard to fathom, but I could not agree with this popular notion in the case of my sister-in-law. Rather, it seemed to me to be an artificial effort made by force; that is; I suspected that she had a deep sense of fear that she might have to spend the rest of her life alone with her daughter. I believe this fear drove her to become a tough and capable person.

My father was very proud of such a daughter-in-law, though to me she appeared as an eternally sorrowful shadow. The reason I did everything I could to support my sister-in-law emotionally was not, I believe, for the sake of my brother. It was from watching the woman's pitiful, sorrowful struggle against fate. My heart was filled with an endless depth of sadness regarding her.

My father's death came unexpectedly, as all such events do.

"S-a-n-g s-u-p. . ." he gasped. Even though he clearly knew

that he was holding my hand, my father closed his eyes for the last time calling my brother's name. His failing voice was like a dying breeze. It echoed from a distant place, winding around every turn of the mountain ridges of the memories of my brother, which had been implanted in my heart.

We found a picture, yellowed with age, and some money in the worn-out, leather wallet which my father carried with him at all times. My brother, wearing his square, college cap, looked out from the picture.

The picture was given to my sister-in-law. She received it gratefully in both her hands and studied it carefully. She then burst into tears, putting her hands to her forehead. It was the first time that she shed tears in front of us on account of my brother.

As if following a pattern set by my father, my mother passed away the next year. I realized keenly for the first time what a wise action my sister-in-law had taken in learning to run my father's business. Although I had once been uncertain as to whether this decision was hers or my father's, I now became confident that my father was responsible for making this wise decision for my sister-in-law. However, I have absolutely no proof that this was so.

After I got married, it was quite natural and necessary for me to leave my parent's home. I refused to take any money from the considerable inheritance left us by my father, though my sister-in-law was anxious to give me half. Finally, I yielded to her wish and received my share, using it as a fund to open my present architectural firm.

Without any help from me, my sister-in-law has managed the store and has raised her daughter, In-hee.

I picked up the white, square envelope that In-hee had left behind.

Miss In-hee
The eldest daughter of
Mr. Sang-sup Park

On a crisp white wedding invitation, my brother came alive as I gazed at his name, imprinted clearly in black letters.

"S-a-n-g s-u-p. . ."

My father's voice was echoing back through every valley of memory which lingered in my heart.

"Y-e-s, F-a-t-h-e-r. . ."

My brother's voice, too, was echoing back from some distant mountain ridge.

At that moment, listening to the two echoes mingle with each other, I sank into a mood of loneliness, assuming the role of the one and only heir of the Park family.

Translated by Hyun-jae Yee Sallee

The Snowy Road

Chung-joon Yee

"**W**e have to leave tomorrow morning."

As I was leaving the breakfast table, I finally managed to blurt out this sentence, which I had been contemplating for some time.

Both my mother and my wife stopped eating and gazed at me blankly.

"Leave tomorrow morning?" my mother echoed in mild shock, as if she could not believe her own ears. She laid her spoon on the table. "You're leaving so soon this time also!"

I decided to clarify my statement, realizing that I had already "spilled the beans."

"Yes, tomorrow morning! I'm not a student on vacation. I can't afford to be idle while others are working hard. Besides, I have a few urgent projects to be taken care of in the office."

"I understand," my mother said. "I wish you could stay here a few more days and get some rest. Since you came down at the peak of this hot weather, I'd hoped you'd stay a few days this time."

"Do you believe I have the luxury of choosing between hot and cold weather?" I complained.

"Must you go back so soon? It is such a long trip back. Do you really have to leave right away? You used to come alone and return at the crack of dawn. I remember it well. But this time you didn't come alone. Please stay one more night and catch up on your needed rest before you leave."

"Well, Mother, I'll enjoy a good rest all day long today. You know that one day's rest means three lost working days for me."

Although travel had been considerably improved, it took a tremendous amount of time to go back and forth between Seoul and my mother's house — one day to get to her house and another day to go back to Seoul.

"I wish you'd take care of urgent matters in the office before you come," my mother said.

This time, my wife, not my mother, looked at me with eyes full of reproach, which indeed had nothing to do with my incompetence in handling office affairs. My wife knew well that no urgent business matters were awaiting my return.

Right before we left Seoul, I told my wife that I had already taken care of every important matter. It was I who suggested to my wife that we take our summer vacation in a relaxed mood this year. I also suggested to her that we visit my mother for a few days during our vacation. My wife was casting resentful looks at me because of my hasty change of plans. She was also reproaching me for my cold decision to leave my mother's home so suddenly. I could clearly detect this, but her gaze also reflected both pity and a pleading that I could not interpret.

"Well, then, if you're that busy, you ought to go back," my mother said. "It won't do any good to hold back a busy person like you. I know you won't listen to me no matter how hard I try to dissuade you from leaving!"

My mother then remained mute for a while, as if she had

finally given up trying to persuade me.

"I know you're always busy," she finally said. "I'd like you to understand me, though. You came all the way down here to see me, yet I couldn't even provide you with a comfortable bed. Please try to understand why I wanted you to stay longer."

My mother began to tamp cheap tobacco into her long pipe. She seemed resigned with no trace of the resentment on her face that I had noted in my wife a few minutes before. She showed no hard feelings toward her heartless son who was anxious to leave his mother in such a hurry. She did not bother to light a match for her pipe. Her face was expressionless.

It was I who was suddenly provoked by her apparent resignation. Annoyed, I stood up briskly. I left the room hastily as if I were pushed out by my mother's expressionless stare. At the edge of the front courtyard near the sliding lattice door, I noticed a small jasmine tree, enduring the scorching sun of noontide.

2.

Behind the house was a grave under the thick-leaved alder tree in the midst of a bean patch that was baked by the intense heat. Seating myself under the shade of the alder tree, where I was almost hidden, I looked down at my mother's one-room hut through the bean bushes. The shape of the house reminded me of a summer mushroom sprouting in a marsh.

I feared that a belated demand for payment of an old debt would emerge suddenly from nowhere at any minute. That damned, dim, humid and tiny one-room hut was to blame in the first place. It was the hut that aroused this terrible sense of nervousness in me. It forced me to feel that my old debt might reappear. It was indeed my mother's hut that had helped me change my mind, deciding to return to Seoul after only one day's stay.

To begin with, I owed nothing to my mother. I prided myself on having a debt-free relationship with her. Consequently, I had nothing to hide from her. My mother's sentiment, of course, was the same about the matter of any debt existing between us.

Noticing that her teeth were completely decayed, I once made a casual suggestion to my mother that I purchase an inexpensive set of dentures for her. She had a terribly difficult time in chewing. But my mother must have doubted my ability to pay for even cheap dentures; she declined my well-intentioned offer right then and there.

"I'm approaching my seventies," she said. "I don't think I have that much time left."

At another time, I recommended she have an operation for her hemorrhoids, which had worsened quite severely. She was in pain whenever she had to go to the bathroom.

"Thank you, son. But, no!" she refused to hear anything further. "I'll go to the other world as I am now. I'm all right. I don't expect any comfort at my age anyway." My mother voiced a reply to my offer very similar to the one concerning the dentures.

"I may be an old woman, but I'm still a decent woman. I can't bring myself to expose my private area to a stranger. I'd rather endure discomfort until my time comes."

It was evident that she had given up on the remainder of her life. She was convinced that she would not live much longer. More precisely, however, my mother felt that she had neither a right to demand nor to receive anything in return from her own son. I thought she understood her position.

I was in the ninth grade when my older brother, a hopeless alcoholic, brought bankruptcy upon our family due to his excessive drinking habits. Finally he died, leaving his three small children and their mother. He also left me a sense of duty because I then became the eldest son in the household.

The relationship between my mother and myself had been like this ever since my brother's death. My mother had not assumed any parental responsibility for me during my high school and college years, or even during my three years of service in the army. Nor had I assumed any filial responsibility for her.

I finished high school and college. Even after I was discharged from the army, I did not dare take up the role of a son toward my mother, not because my mother did not deserve such treatment,but because I just could not afford to do so. In the long run, I ended up neglecting the responsibility that my deceased brother had left for me to assume. I had no choice but to neglect my duty as the eldest son in the family.

Thus, my relationship with my mother was one in which nothing was ever given or received. My mother knew it well, more than anyone else. Therefore, she could not nurture any hope or harbor any resentment towards me. Such, I thought, was our understanding.

This time, however, I detected a somewhat different attitude in my mother, who had once flatly refused my help, for her own benefit, to obtain dentures or to undergo an operation. My mother, only two years shy of eighty now, was in the last stage of her life. All of a sudden, though, she must have had a certain, renewed appetite for life. I suspected she was dreaming an impossible dream. It was, indeed, a preposterous dream. "The Movement for the Replacement of Old Roofs" was the beginning of the trouble.

"Every house in the village has had its roof replaced with either tiles or plastic slates," my mother had said offhandedly as if she were merely gossiping. This happened last night right before the three of us — my mother, my wife, and myself went to bed. As night deepened, my sister-in-law and her children had left to sleep at a neighbor's house. After they left, the three of us took out the bedding and prepared to go to sleep in that tiny one bedroom hut.

It was then we heard the night workers' chorus — "hi-ho, hi-ho" — resounding loudly, from somewhere not very far away. I strained my ears with curiosity, trying to make out the sound. I asked my mother to explain its meaning.

"The whole village is remodeling their houses, as if competing with one another," my mother explained lightly as if she just happened to remember it. "They work through the night, making such a fuss, you know."

According to my mother, the village people were doing their part to improve their old roofs, honoring the campaign of roof improvement throughout the farming and fishing villages. Since Unification, it had been very difficult for the villagers to replace their roofs with either tiles or slates because of poor harvests. My mother informed us that brand rice seeds were distributed by the government throughout the entire village.

The ambitious task of replacing the old roofs had been going rather well in every aspect since early spring. According to my mother, if any householder completed his roof according to government regulations, he would receive fifty-thousand won from the government as a subsidy. My mother said most of the villagers replaced their roofs during the slack season right before and right after the period of transplanting rice seedlings into the rice paddies.

When I was told for the first time all about this movement, my heart sank deeply. At that moment, the idea of owing something to my mother popped into my head. What if she nurtured a futile hope for her dream of a better life? I managed to overcome my anxiety, however. My mother would not demand anything hasty or unreasonable from a son like myself. I had trusted and depended on my mother's character for a long time. Even if she did nurture the impossible hope of a new roof for her house, it was out of the question due to the condition of her hut. To begin with, the house was not strong enough to hold the weight of new tiles or slates on the roof.

I suspected my mother knew this too and, therefore, could not possibly have any hope for the improvement. The way she talked about it gave me the impression that she was merely referring to someone else's business. However, I found out that I was wrong. I had misunderstood her all along. Her deep inner thought was quite different from mine.

"If this movement is sponsored by the local government, I'm sure you've been told about it several times." I made this insensitive remark out of over-optimism. Soon, however, I realized my mistake. My mother got up from her bedding and began to fill her long pipe, over her pillow, with a pinch of cheap tobacco.

"What makes you think my house was excluded?" my mother said in a matter-of-fact tone of voice, as if she were still conveying somebody's message. "The head of our village came and pressed me to go along with the movement. The men from the town office came and threatened me also. It happened once or twice. In the end, however, the authorities changed their tactics by pleading for my help, so to speak."

"How did you manage to hold onto your excuses, Mother." I asked. I still could not figure out what she was really thinking.

"There's nothing to make excuses about," she replied. "They also have good eyes to see for themselves. If they pleaded with me, I did the same. I told them that even if I am an old woman, I am a human being who has a desire to live in better conditions. I told them I'd love to have my roof replaced with new tiles. I also told them I'd love to have new pillars. Well, it can be done only in my imagination. I invited them to look closely at my hut. I told them the house is nothing but a hut made of clay. How can anyone put tiles on the roof, I asked."

"And then what happened?"

"Well, after that, they came a few more times. Then they stopped coming and nagging altogether. They must know what pathetic conditions I live in. They're not so stupid as not to notice the degree of poverty I endure. Once they saw my house, they knew." My mother stopped talking and pushed the end of the hot pipe with her calloused, weather-beaten thumb-tip.

"I bet the villagers wanted an exemplary village after completing the roof replacement one hundred percent," I said uncomfortably, hoping to end the conversation. But again, I miscalculated.

"Incidentally, the authorities said the same thing as you just did," my mother replied. "After they finish the house they're working on tonight, all the houses in the village will be completed except two, mine and Soon-sim's down the road."

"Nonetheless, do you really think the authorities will keep hounding you to put new tiles on your roof just because they're anxious to make this village a model for the sake of the movement?"

"I don't know, son. If they asked me only to replace the roof, I would be tempted to comply with their wishes. However, to begin with, this house needs to be rebuilt. It needs stronger pillars to support the tiles, I tell you."

Somehow the conversation had lost track of its original subject, a model village. Realizing this, my heart sank once again. It was too late to change the topic, however.

"The core of this movement is replacing the roof only," my mother continued. "But some people have taken advantage of this opportunity and actually remodeled their houses."

My mother went on to tell me in detail about the entire village. Listening to her, I realized that this movement had indeed much flexibility. Its initial purpose was to replace the thatched roofs with either tiles or slates. However, as the task proceeded, a number of households found their houses structurally unable to hold the weight of the tiles. In order to sustain the weight of a new tile roof, they had to replace the old pillars.

Using this as an excuse, the majority of the villagers ended up remodeling their houses by expanding the original foundation. My mother was asked to do the same. The poor condition of the old pillar was just an excuse, they felt. Just three households persisted in not complying with the flow of the movement, using their shoddy pillars as an excuse. One of these three families, however, gave in and was working on the new foundation tonight. She added that they would work through the night.

I did not believe my mother's refusal to put new tiles on the roof stemmed from the need for new pillars. It was rather from her fear of also needing a new foundation, which I believe had made her abandon the idea altogether.

I could not, as yet, afford to be optimistic about this situation.

Suddenly, I was enveloped once again with a sense of concern. Perhaps I did owe something to my mother. As I was lost in thought, my mother seemed to shift her interest to the waning glow in her tobacco pipe.

"This time the town office people let it go without making such a big deal for me," my mother began again, seemingly talking to herself since I gave her no response whatsoever. "Anyway, I wonder if they'll be as lenient with me next year as they have been so far. I don't like to think that I'd comply with their wish out of fear. Nonetheless, think of your nephews, niece, and your sister-in-law. They may not like to sleep with me in the same room. Even though there is enough room, every night they go to one of the neighbors' to sleep. Perhaps they can't stand the smell of an old woman. I just can't ignore their sleeping at someone else's house."

Listening to my mother, I could detect a considerable, detailed agenda of plans that had already been filed in her head.

"The government will offer fifty-thousand won as a subsidy, mind you," she continued. "If I decided to go along with the movement, I doubt I would have to spend a great deal of money just to finish the roof. I realize I might have a hard time finding workers since I have no male adult members in my household, unlike other families. However, if your sister-in-law promised to work in the fields during the summer for the neighbor right across from my house, I don't think the man could entirely ignore our labor problem. I'm sure he'd help us."

My mother added that she could ask this neighbor for help doing the clay work. She could also ask about buying timber for new pillars from the head of the village at a bargain price since he owned the valley.

The glow of her pipe had now died away. She kept on puffing the extinguished pipe as she talked about how difficult it was for her to give up the government subsidy of fifty-thousand won and the would-be help from the neighbors, but she gave no sign of dissatisfaction with me. In fact, she also asked nothing from me.

She discussed all this as if it had taken place long ago and she was merely expressing idle thoughts, certainly not expecting her desire to become a reality. But I could tell that my mother was going out of her way not to relieve me of any sense of burden.

She silently puffed on the cold pipe. Finally, she heaved a gentle sigh, as if having difficulty in repressing her hidden desire any longer.

"Taking this opportunity, I was tempted to add an extra room and replace the old roof with slates if I could," she said, sighing again. "I don't know when I'll die. Perhaps today or tomorrow. Anyway, my life span, of no more worth than that of a wild animal, seems to be long. My head is now crowded with wild notions." Then my mother at last disclosed her inner desire. "I don't have a room for even a single chest," she continued. "Whenever I see the chest being pushed from one place to another, I'm tempted to carry out my desire to add a room and put on a new roof."

My mother succeeded by this unique method in revealing with crystal clarity her innermost hope. She apparently had felt such a desire at one time, but surely she did not cherish it now. I did not know what to say then. I was in bed, listening to her with my eyes closed, reminding myself again and again that I owed nothing to my mother. To the end, she successfully maintained a most unique tone of absolute resignation.

"It's all useless," my mother said softly. "If the world ran as smoothly as one desired, who wouldn't be sorry about getting old! I have heard people say the old are like children. Perhaps I am becoming too old. I think like a child now."

In the end, my mother blamed her old age and hopeless senility for her secret, innermost desire. Despite this, there was no way for me to fail to discern her thoughts. Even my wife, listening to my mother without stirring in her bed, pretending to sleep, must have clearly recognized my mother's real wish.

As she brought a basin full of water for me to wash my face and hands the next morning, she asked me reproachfully,

"Couldn't you have said something better to your mother last night?" I threw a scowling, harsh glance at her as a message not to put her nose where it didn't belong. Unaffected by my glare, my wife proceeded to reprimand me harshly.

"You're so cruel," she cried. "How could you find it in your heart to be so aloof? Don't you feel sorry for your old mother? You could have said something comforting to her!"

I saw clearly that my wife understood exactly what my mother had tried to convey to me. She was more concerned about my mother than I was. I was sure that my wife had already sensed in detail all of the deepest thoughts I had concerning my mother. My wife's earnest anger toward my decision to return to Seoul the next morning in such a hurry was mainly because she knew and understood how shamefully I had treated my mother.

In any event, what could she have done to change things, I wondered, and felt resigned. It was evident that my mother wished to have her house remodeled. I could not fathom her reasoning. I wondered how she could forget that I was not indebted to her for anything at all. As my mother suggested earlier, she must indeed have entered into a state of senility. Is it really true that an old person transforms into a baby?

My mother had apparently aged so much that she was unable to distinguish between pride and honor. I had no reason to feel guilt because of her senility. The only important thing for me to remember was that I owed her nothing. Whether she became brazen or senile, I did not care. All that mattered was keeping my position of being debt-free to my mother.

"I owe her nothing. I absolutely don't!" I reassured myself. "That's why Mother has no heart to ask me directly for her desire to remodel her house. I know she knows that I'm debt-free to her."

As I was thinking about this, I heard the steady, lazy cries of the cicada from somewhere. As if reinforced with confidence, I stood up resolutely from the shady spot beneath the alder tree. Below the bean patch, the panorama of the entire village came into focus, as a bird's-eye view from the hill where I stood. As my mother said, the only thatched roofs in the village belonged to my mother's mushroom-shaped hut and another house down the road.

"Damn it!" I cursed. "Why the hell is the government making such a fuss over this movement of improving roofs at a time like this!"

Disturbed, I cursed the improvement program.

3.

Quite some time after the sun sank, I climbed down the hill, crossed the bean patch and walked into the backyard of my mother's house.

"I'm not expecting to live very long," my mother was saying to my wife. "Of course, I do not expect such a thing as a comfortable life at my age. I didn't mean to have my roof replaced with tiles or add an extra room for my sake. I suppose my wish was too unreal. I'm worried about them after I die. I'm not greedy just because I want to have things done before my time. I'd like to do something for them."

As I was about to enter the front courtyard, my mother's low voice could be faintly heard from the room through the half-open sliding lattice-door. I was overhearing a conversation that I instinctively knew I would rather not hear.

"If it were considerably cooler in the spring or fall, or even if it were cooler in the summertime when people can sleep under a canopy in the courtyard, I wouldn't be so much concerned," my mother went on. "However, what if I die in the dead of winter, which would be just my luck. My daughter-in-law and her children would have no choice but to keep my body in the upper part of the only room we have in the house. Then, what are they going to do in that situation?"

So my mother was still talking about the house! Was my wife's anger toward me so deep because I had behaved so objectionably and remained so aloof? Was that why she was shrewd enough to talk to my mother directly? It was plain to me that my wife had managed to succeed in leading my mother to continue talking. Now my mother was wholeheartedly expressing her wish about the house right in front of my wife, who must have won my mother's trust. My mother was unveiling clearly the story behind her wish. The transparency of her desire was presented right before my eyes, when I was already to pass by it one way or another. I had felt that her resignation had become a long-time habit, believing this shielded me against any sense of shame.

Although I had guessed her wish long before, I was quite unprepared for hearing this very clear statement from her. I watched the last ray of hope disappear. There was one thing about her statement that clarified things for me at last. This was her own personal reason for her sudden and preposterous desire to improve her house. My mother was not motivated by the idea of enjoying a new comfortable life for herself, but for those who would be left behind after her death.

"Even though I came here as an outsider, I've spoken ill of no one or hurt no one in this village to this day. I've lived in this decent way all of my life." My mother was speaking to my wife again. "I can't deny that I have been leading an extremely meager life. As you can see, I'm still living in a poverty-stricken condition. Nonetheless, no one in the neighborhood has said anything unkind to me. I have come this far, keeping a decent relationship with my neighbors. Do you understand what I'm trying to say, my dear? After I die, the villagers will come to the burial ground either to cast a shovelful of dirt on my coffin or to put some grass on my grave. I'm sure that is the least they would do for me. Who would prevent these mourners, regardless of age, young or old, from paying their last respects to me? There is nothing more tiring for people than fulfilling their duties after someone's death. No one can prevent people from paying a last homage, especially to an old woman who has known nothing but poverty all her life."

She sighed deeply and continued, "Do you believe it's a crime for me to want to treat these mourners with just a glass of cheap whiskey? So, I suppose, I came up with this wild idea after considerable thinking. When I take my last breath of life, if my body cannot be buried the same day, it will be a big problem. You see, the body and the rest of the family have to stay in the same room. Besides that, what about you and your husband who will come down here from such a long distance? Considering all this, that's why I had this notion to have an extra room added in any way I could manage. I just need a small room that can shield us from the cold wind and hold a small person like me. Anyway, my wish stayed only in my heart. I guess it was nothing but a futile hope of a senile old woman. I must be living in a fantasy world. Do you think I am?"

My mother's wish, I realized, had originated as preparation for her own death. I could understand the reason behind it. Ever since she was forced to leave her own village and wander from one village to another after the family's bankruptcy, my mother had been obsessed with the idea of making preparations for her own death. She had already secured a gravesite (she called it a homesite) from a certain elderly man in this present village. It was located on a sunny side of the foot of the mountain that overlooked the village. She often went to her gravesite to enjoy a sun-bath on a fine day, even in wintertime. I could tell she was now making precise final preparations for her imminent death.

I found myself feeling awkward. I wanted to leave the spot as quietly as I possibly could. But as I was about to take a step to leave the place, I overheard a remark of my wife's that changed the subject abruptly.

"I understand your previous house was big and built on a huge lot." Perhaps she could not control her curiosity any longer; or perhaps she was desperate to find something to comfort my mother and happened to think of this statement. She might have wanted my mother to reminisce over the fond memory of having the spacious house that she once enjoyed and thus somehow be consoled.

Also, my wife, such a good soul, undoubtedly sensed my mother's shame at revealing her obvious poverty to her daughter-in-law. Recalling her former position might soothe my mother's injured pride to some degree.

I found the need to leave, diminished for the time being.

"My old house was spacious. Very, very big, you know," I overheard my mother say. "It was enormous. The front and back yards put together were as big as a regular playground. Well, it doesn't matter, now. It's all useless. Someone else has lived in that house now for more than twenty years."

"I know how you must feel, Mother," my wife said. "I'm sure your fond memories about your big, splendid house stay in your heart. You can recall those good, happy days whenever you feel irritated or depressed about your present house."

"What's the use of recalling the memory, my dear? Whenever I think of those bygone years, my already troubled heart becomes even more burdened. I don't need to refresh my memory now."

"You may be right, Mother. I don't blame you for becoming more irritable in your present living conditions whenever your memory returns to those days in such a huge house. I feel bad that you have ended up living in a tiny, one-room hut."

Was the intent of their conversation to complain or to comfort? As I had been listening to them for quite some time, I began once again to doubt my wife's true motive. I could tell by the tone of her voice that my wife was not trying to comfort my mother. She was, in fact, provoking my mother, whose heart had become subsequently more troubled.

My wife was indeed fanning my mother's guarded desire to remodel the house by forcing her to expose that desire. I now believed this was my wife's intention. My first assumption concerning my wife's motive was turning out to be not so terribly wrong.

"By the way, Mother, why don't you move this chest out of the room and store it elsewhere? It takes up too much space in this tiny room." My wife, at last, led the subject into a most uncomfortable matter, which I had been avoiding to this day. Namely, it was the story behind the chest.

It was either seventeen or eighteen years ago. I was in the tenth grade. My brother's heavy drinking habits worsened as each day passed. He sold every rice paddy and vegetable field we owned. He even sold the mountain that we had inherited from our ancestors. My brother sold everything we had in order to support his alcoholism. One day I heard a rumor that my brother sold our house as a last resort. We had lived in that house since my father's generation.

At that time, I was living in a nearby city and spending my winter vacation there. I could not stand not knowing what in the world was going on back home. In order to kill this nagging curiosity, I went to the village where I used to live before I went back to school. According to the rumor I heard, the house had already been sold. Consequently, I did not expect to find any member of my family in the house. Although I was prepared for this, I had no place to go to find out the whereabouts of my family.

I waited until dusk gathered before I actually entered the street where I used to live. The situation, as had been rumored in the city, existed unmistakably. The house was completely empty. I could find no one around. I left and went to see a distant relative who lived nearby.

According to my relative, my mother was still waiting for me in the house. It was unexpected news for me.

"Why are you acting like that in our own street? Where do you think you are? This is your house, remember?" my mother reproached me as I appeared to be hesitant, not knowing how to behave myself near the house. I was standing awkwardly near the gate when she came up to me. She must have somehow heard about my visit to my distant relative.

I followed my mother inside, still hoping something advantageous would happen. Betraying my last ray of hope, however, I could sense easily that our house had been sold as I entered the main wing of the house. On that evening, my mother prepared a meal for me as she used to. She and I spent the night there, and she sent me back to the city at the break of dawn.

Later I managed to find out that my mother had secured permission from the new owner of the house for her to fix dinner for me and have me spend one last night in our house. She had been awaiting my visit to our house so that she could carry out her wish for my sake. I suspected she wanted me to sleep, even if for one last night, in our own house, feeling comfortable in a familiar environment.

Although a strangeness in the air told me the house had been sold, my mother was keeping it mopped and dusted. My mother's chest and simple bedding remained in the same corner of the main bedroom.

At dawn, when I was ready to leave for the city, my mother finally told me in her clear tone of voice that our house was sold. It was evident that she wanted to comfort me and believed in her heart that the mere existence of the chest in the room might help me recall the atmosphere of our old house to which I was accustomed.

My mother had now been storing the chest for nearly twenty years. I believed the reason for this was the scarcity of her belongings as she had to keep moving from one place to another. The chest always made me feel uncomfortable. While I could firmly convince myself that I owed my mother nothing, whenever I looked at the chest, I felt very awkward, as if I were facing an indebtedness I did not intend to acknowledge.

Such was the chest to me.

On this visit, the chest succeeded in making me feel this way again. The first moment I walked into my mother's room, the sight of the chest caused me a sense of discomfort. The deep root of my final decision to leave for Seoul after only one day's stay, I reasoned, was due to the chest.

I had told my wife the history of this chest several times. If my wife understood the meaning of the chest, I was confident she would understand how I felt about it. Moreover, if she knew I could overhear their conversation near the room, she would surely be even more sympathetic to my feelings. Nevertheless, I found myself so tense that I nearly resorted to my old habit of picking my nose to calm myself.

I was seized with tension. I was afraid of suddenly encountering a past-due debt popping out of nowhere. My mother might attack in her shameful way, cornering me with the dilemma of admitting this old debt.

"You can do whatever you like. Even if you insist, I am sure I owe you nothing. Not a thing! You might try desperately, Mother, but it's useless. Nothing can make me believe I owe you anything. I am debt-free." I closed my eyes as if I were praying and recited this over and over. And I waited. Again, I overheard my mother replying to my wife.

"If I move the chest somewhere else, where can we keep our clothing?" My mother was talking in her usual matter-of-fact, almost casual tone. Somehow this relieved my anxiety. "Besides, we have no other place to store the chest!"

"You could hang your clothes on nails on the wall," my wife suggested. "Most of all, a person needs space to lie down with one's legs fully stretched out. It appears to me that you treasure the chest more than the well-being of people."

My wife's bold remark was obviously intended to test my mother's deep attachment to the chest. In spite of my wife's urging, however, my mother responded in her usual manner.

"I'm afraid you don't know what you're talking about," my mother said. "If we don't have even that chest, who can tell this is a house with someone living in it. It belongs right here in the house. Don't you see that it testifies to the presence of people?"

"I bet you must have some kind of meaningful, hidden story about your chest," my wife teased. "Did you buy it when you were first married?"

My mother was old enough to be my wife's grandmother.

Often, my wife acted and talked rather disrespectfully around my mother as if she were a privileged granddaughter. This time, to be sure, my wife was even mischievous.

"What story, my dear, could you be talking about?" My mother seemed not to wish to talk about the chest any further.

"How did your house come to be sold, Mother?"

"What kind of question is that, how the house came to be sold? I didn't sell it in the spirit of playing a game. I suppose I'm not destined to have my own house." My mother did not have the slightest idea that my wife knew all about the reason for that sale.

"But, Mother, there must have been some reason why you had to sell your house," my wife insisted. "I understand your husband went to a lot of trouble to have that house built and died while it was under construction."

"You're right, my dear. We could have the house only after going through a lot of hard times. You see, the house was not built all at once as others were. We added one room at a time as our income increased in the course of many years. Such was our house. And now it has ended up in someone else's hands. Anyway, what's the use of talking about it now? I tell you the house was not meant for me. That's why the house went to somebody else. It's useless to talk about it."

"I can see your point. By the same token, you must be more acutely sorry about it since your house was made possible after such hardships, especially when you think of your present living conditions. Please tell me what happened at that time. What really made you sell your house?"

"Stop it, my dear. It's all futile. It was a long time ago, and my memory is not so good anymore."

My mother tried desperately not to yield to my wife's persistent efforts to entice her into telling the whole story.

"All right, Mother. You must be worried that your troubles might unnecessarily hurt me. Even if you are, Mother, it won't help now. Do you want to know the truth? I have known about your house all this time."

My wife was not the kind of woman to be discouraged and retreat just because of my mother's sudden silence. As my mother closed her mouth, my wife also remained silent for a few moments. Her silence, however, was short-lived.

"Anyway, Mother, I feel for you," my wife went on. "Your heart must be very troubled. You should have kept your old house at any cost, Mother. By the way, what was the story behind selling the house?"

My wife's inquiry was not innocent. Just as she knew all about the history of my mother's chest, my wife also had full knowledge of why the house had been sold. Still she kept trying to have my mother repeat the whole story. She was trying to find out what lay behind my mother's desire, using the story of the house to achieve her scheme. My wife's persistent effort only drew out my mother's stubborn side.

"I know not only the story behind the sale of your house, but I also know how you managed to have your son spend the last night in the house that had already been sold. I know it all. I've been pretending that I knew nothing. I was told you still kept your worn-out chest even to the last night in the house, trying to give your son the impression that you still lived there as if nothing had happened."

"You heard? From whom?" My mother asked, in a tone of mild shock.

"From that person, of course," my wife replied. Although I had not been certain that my wife sensed my presence, at last I could tell for sure, since she was referring to me as "that person." My wife, I guessed, had been aware of my presence all along.

"Please, Mother, tell me everything. Why don't you let it out once and for all? Why do you keep it all inside? We're your children. Why must you hide it from your children and bury everything in your heart?"

My wife sounded nearly tearful. My mother remained speechless for a good while as if she did not know what to say next. In the meantime, my mouth became extremely dry. I could not breathe properly as I waited, wondering if she were going to respond to my wife's plea.

Ignoring my wife's and my anguished waiting, however, my mother replied in a voice controlled to the end: "I wonder how he managed to remember the last night in the house for this long!"

"You're right, Mother. He still remembers it. When he paced around the house, not knowing exactly what to do, you took him inside and even prepared a meal for him, trying to convince him that the house hadn't been sold."

"Well, you seem to know it all. Then, my dear, why are you deliberately pressing so hard for me to recall and repeat those days?"

"Because he has already begun to forget about it. Besides, I can't hear the truth from him. He's so aloof that he willfully forgets things like that. So, I'd like to hear the truth from you personally this time. Not his version of the story, but your very own — your honest sentiments on that last night in your house!"

"What about my sentiments, my dear? I have no particularly different story to tell you than what you've already been told. I sold the house by necessity, not by choice. Under the circumstances, it was the only way. Although I had to do it, I couldn't entirely forget the house. My son was hesitant about whether he should go into the house when I found him."

Unable to bear my wife's insistence, my mother finally spoke reluctantly, reminiscing about that last night in our old house. Her tone of voice carried none of her sentiments on that distant night.

"I scolded him for being so timid around his own house and I took him inside immediately. I prepared a hot meal for him and had him spend the night there. Before dawn, I sent him back," my mother continued."

"How did you feel at that time, Mother?"

"Well, speaking of my feelings then," my mother said, "I wanted to have him spend the night in the house even if it was already sold. My desire was so acute that I swept the courtyard and mopped the floor while coming and going back and forth to the road, waiting for him to come, you see. I felt great relief when I fulfilled my wish to offer him a hot meal and warm bed. I was well-pleased."

"You're saying that you sent your son off in a satisfied mood. Am I not right, Mother? Nonetheless, were you really happy to send him off like that? Were you truly pleased, Mother? What I'm trying to say is, your son had a place to which he could go back – his school. But, what about you? You had no decent place to go."

"What are you trying to get from me this time?" my mother asked sheepishly.

"I'd like to hear about your genuine feelings when you sent your young son off to a school in a strange town the way you did. And yet you had no place to live and had to move from one place to another. So, I'd like to hear your true sentiments about your experiences during those days."

"It's all futile. You might as well forget the idea. Even if I tell you, how can you possibly understand how I really felt then, my dear?"

My mother remained reticent. I suspected that she had been nourishing the story deep inside her heart. I found myself impatient now, not being able to wait any longer.

I had to intervene right then and there to stop my mother from talking. Even if my wife aggressively insisted upon having her way, I knew my mother well and knew she would not want me to find out about that night. If I were present, I knew the conversation between them could not continue, especially on my mother's part.

I made a dry coughing sound and presented myself abruptly in front of the sliding lattice door on which my mother's eyes were fixed.

4.

The danger seemed to pass. When supper was served, I was especially provided with a bottle of rice wine by my mother, as she had always done for me. For some reason, she did not appear to be a bit concerned about my drinking in spite of my late brother's abusive drinking habit, which eventually destroyed our family. Whenever I visited my mother, without fail, she bought a gallon of rice wine and then served it with her own hands.

"Have a glass of wine and go to sleep." Thus, my mother always offered me a drink and wished me a good night's sleep afterwards. She did exactly the same thing on that evening.

"Do you really have to leave tomorrow morning?" my mother asked carefully as we sat around the dinner table, trying to discern my real intention.

"Yes, I have to go to take care of some matters," I replied bluntly in an unnecessarily angry tone of voice. At my response, my mother seemed totally resigned.

"I understand, son. Why don't you have wine with your meal and retire early?" My mother advised me to go to bed early because I had to leave early for the long trip back to Seoul. Without uttering a single word, I obeyed her. I emptied nearly a half-gallon of wine with my supper. And, as if I could not overcome the influence of the wine, I went to bed quite early. After my sister-in-law and her children left to find a place to sleep elsewhere, my mother, my wife, and I lay in the room again as we had the previous night.

I felt I had managed to have those nearly critical hours come to an end. I shut my eyes. Once I awoke from my sleep the next morning, I calculated, the visit would come to an end as I wished. I did not need to worry about the roof business, the chest, or anything else for that matter. I wondered whether or not my mother had a hidden bill that was due from me. If I spent this night safely, her due bill, if any, would become waste paper for good.

"I'll try to go to sleep. Debt or not, everything will be all right once I fall asleep. How could I owe her anything, anyway?" I told myself this, trying to invite the nymph of sleep. I was in quite a free and easy spirit. It must have been the wine. Heavy drowsiness swept over me immediately, closing my eyelids.

I wandered in and out of a hazy sleep for some time before my drowsiness slowly lifted from me. I had no idea what had driven my sleepiness away. Even in my light sleep, I could vaguely hear my mother murmuring softly.

"On that night, we had a sudden, unusually heavy snow fall," my mother was saying. "I tried to sleep, but failed. Finally, I managed to sleep a few hours. When I woke up around daybreak, the entire world seemed to be covered with brilliant snow. The snow didn't stop me, though. I busied myself fixing breakfast, which warmed us. As soon as we finished our meal, we left in a hurry on a snow-covered road."

Suddenly, my mind became quite clear. It was beyond my belief that my mother was in the midst of finally disclosing to my wife the story of that night in our old house.

"Under normal circumstances, we could have left after sunrise," my mother said. "I was still ashamed of my situation. I cursed my fate. However, I had no choice. Before dawn, my son and I were on the snowy road. It was nearly fifteen miles to the marketplace in town. It was a long walk along the mountain road, I tell you!"

My mother was revealing that day moment by moment. She talked gently as if she were speaking to her little grandchild about an old tale. The way she talked gave me the sensation of snuggling down in bed to hear, as a child does, an elder's reminiscences. My wife had finally succeeded in leading my mother to disclose her feelings.

"Even if I tell you, my dear, how can you possibly comprehend how I felt?" My mother paused before she resumed. "It was still dark. We slid and fell as we walked on the rough, slippery mountain road. However, we managed to arrive at the bus terminal on

time." My mother was telling my wife about the night, no, the dawn, when she had accompanied me to the bus terminal. I had never, even once, told my wife about this particular event. I had desperately wanted to forget that snowy road, wishing it would somehow disappear from my memory.

To my dismay, my mother was now going back to the past in her subdued voice as if she were mentioning an old debt that could never be repaid in any way. As I listened to my mother, events of that day finally unfolded their wings in my head as distinctly as if I could touch them. Was my mother overwhelmed by her sense of sorrow for me, her young son? She had no alternative but to carry out what she had to do under the circumstances.

At first, she offered to accompany me only to where I would leave the village. Then she insisted upon accompanying me onto the side road that led from the village to the mountain. Even after we climbed the mountain pass, she insisted that we walk the path together until the newly constructed road appeared. Whenever she insisted upon accompanying me a longer distance, we ended up having an argument. Except for these slight altercations, we said nothing to each other.

It would have been a lot better if we had left the village after the sun had risen. Yet neither of us dared to leave after daybreak. All things considered, we found it preferable to leave the village before the veil of darkness lifted.

As my mother had mentioned to my wife previously, we walked, slid, and fell often on that snowy road. When I fell, my mother would help me get up and vice versa. In this manner, we emerged on the big road in silence. Even from that point, a considerable distance remained before we reached the bus terminal near the town office. My mother and I ended up walking along the big road all the way to the terminal. It was still not daybreak.

I do not recall what happened to us after that. I got on the bus and saw my mother walking back to the village on the snowy road in the darkness. That was everything I remembered. My memory stopped right there. I had never been told how my mother managed to return to the village after she saw me off at the bus station. From the moment I got on the bus, leaving my mother all alone, I did not want to think of her. She had never uttered a single word to me about what happened to her after that early dawn.

Today, for some reason, she was recalling every moment of that morning.

"After we managed to enter the streets of the marketplace, we hurried on until we saw the bus terminal in the distance. The bus was about to leave the garage. I waved my arm frantically to stop it. All drivers must be cold-hearted or very impatient. Anyway, the bus driver barely stopped the bus and swiftly took my son away. He disappeared from my sight, only leaving a clanking noise behind."

"So what did you do afterwards, Mother?" my wife asked at last after listening to my mother in silence.

Suddenly, I was afraid of my mother's continued tale. I was tempted to get up from my bedding and prevent her from talking any further. Even though the possibility existed in my mind, my limbs wouldn't cooperate. My whole body sank into the depth of the sea, making me feel heavy as if I were water-logged cotton. I could not move my body in any direction. The sense of a certain sweet sorrow, or sweet fatigue, that was beyond description, hazily embraced me.

"What do you think I did, my dear? Like a person who has lost her senses, I stood still in the darkness by the roadside for a good while, staring at the road where the bus disappeared. How can I put it into proper words how empty I felt then?" My mother still spoke calmly in her controlled tone of voice, as if she were still reminiscing about a past from which she was emotionally far removed.

"I don't know how long I stood there like that," my mother continued. "My senses came back somewhat as the cold wind licked my face. When I thought of returning to the village, I was gripped with a new sense of emptiness. Before he left, he and I had walked along the rough road together. When I was reminded that I, an old woman, had to go back alone, I couldn't make myself return. To make matters worse, it was still dark. So, I went inside the bus terminal and sat down on a wooden chair, resting my forehead on my knees. After nearly an hour, the eastern sky began to lighten. Even though I didn't have to make haste, I started to walk back hurriedly. I don't think I'll ever forget that early morning as long as I live."

"Do you mean the time when you had to go back to the village alone?" my wife asked.

"As I walked alone along the same snowy road we had walked on before, not one footprint was on it besides our own. Not a single soul had passed by since then. On the snowy road, I could see our footprints, side by side, still distinctively imprinted on the newly-built road where the snowfall had stopped."

"You must have missed him very much merely looking at his footprints, Mother," my wife commented thoughtfully.

"You're right about that, my dear. I missed him so much. More than I can describe! I passed by the end of the big road and entered the winding mountain road. Even then I could see his prints. I felt both his warm body temperature and his friendly voice in them. Whenever wild pigeons flew by noisily, I wondered if my son's soul was returning to me as a pigeon. I was also confused as I looked at the snow-clad trees, as if he would appear anytime from behind them. As I was walking in that frame of mind, my dear, along the winding, lonesome mountain road, I only followed his footprints in the snow. 'Oh, my son, my son — now I, this wretched old woman, am returning all alone after sending you off, taking this same road you and I walked together.' I said this, you see."

"Did you cry at that moment?"

"Yes, I did indeed. I did more than cry. I wept ceaselessly over his clear footprints. I wept for his every step. I wished him the very best, calling to him, 'Oh my son, my son, please stay healthy. Please live a good, comfortable life. I hope you'll receive many blessings even if only you are left among my family.' I prayed for his promising future in my tears. I wept until my eyes blurred."

My mother's story seemed to be nearly over now. My wife was speechless as if she did not know what to say next.

"Anyhow, although I took a good long time walking aimlessly, I managed to reach the mountainside behind the village. As I had no reason to make haste, I couldn't bring myself to enter the village immediately. So I cleared the snow from a place on the path and sat there for a long while."

"You didn't have any place to go back to then, did you, Mother?"

My wife, who had remained silent for some time, asked this as if she were unable to keep her silence any longer. Her tearful tone of voice was now trembling with emotion. I, likewise, could not endure my mother's story any longer. I wanted to intervene. I was exceedingly troubled about her response to my wife's question. I could not bear listening to her reply, although I knew well it was impossible for me to avoid it. I was still unable to open my eyes. I simply could not open them under the light, or get up. It was not just the sinking sensation that gave me total paralysis of my limbs. Nor, was it any lingering drowsiness that prevented me from getting up. The reason was that I could not show the warm tears that soaked my eyelids to my mother or my wife. I was too ashamed.

Abruptly my wife shook me with force, causing me to become wide awake. "Please get up, dear, and say something. Please!" she urged as if she already knew of my emotion. The tone of her voice was near crying. Despite her effort, I did not get up. I shut my eyes more tightly to hold back surging tears. I pretended to sleep soundly.

"Let him be. Don't bother him. He's sleeping so soundly, and he needs the rest since he's leaving early tomorrow morning," my mother said calmly. Only my mother did not lose self-control.

"Anyway, you're mistaken about one thing," my mother concluded in her composed and somewhat nostalgic voice as if she were still talking about some old, half-forgotten tale. "The reason

I couldn't leave the mountain passage and enter the village right away wasn't because I had no place to go once I got to the village. As long as I'm alive, I'll be capable of taking care of myself. You see, I had already managed to secure a small rented room for myself. It was the blinding morning sunlight, not the uncertainty of finding a place to live. The whole village was then showered with blissful sunlight. I could not even look at the snow-covered roof of our old house because of the sunlight. To make the matter worse, all the chimneys throughout the village were smoking from fires of breakfasts being prepared. How could I dare walk into the village, feeling so ashamed? I couldn't face direct sunlight in this frame of mind. The bright sunlight shamed me so much that I couldn't even attempt to take one single step. I merely sat there, thoughtfully, hoping to adjust my eyes to the blinding rays of light. . ."

Translated by Hyun-jae Yee Sallee

Winter Outing

Wan-suh Park

I immersed myself in the hot-spring bath. Instead of enjoying myself, I thought of something disgusting — was this water really from a natural spring?

The shower head and the faucets marked "hot" and "cold" attached to an ordinary tiled wall looked almost the same as those in any other shabby hotel. The bathroom of this room in the second-class hotel where I was staying did not impress me. I saw no evidence that the hot water pouring from the red-marked faucet was natural, hot-spring water gushing forth from the ground; nor could I prove it was simply ordinary hot tap water.

I had no chronic disease requiring a hot-spring treatment, nor any faith in its effect. Some people believed that it was beneficial, others did not. I was determined to find fault with the water, yet doing so put me in a melancholy mood.

The purpose of this trip was not for pleasure. I had decided to come here on the spur of the moment, prodded by an internal conflict. I really did not care whether or not my trip became a disaster.

Although my artist husband was not famous in a commercial sense, he was recognized by art critics for the unique quality of his paintings. He was considered a major artist, possessing a modest number of admirers.

Lately, he had been preparing for his third private exhibition. He was so busy that he frequently stayed in his downtown studio. Concerned about his health, I often took food to his studio. My husband dropped by our home only briefly to change his clothes.

The day before I left on my trip, I had gone downtown and bought some tender, pre-cooked roast beef for him before I went to his studio. His married daughter was already there. My husband was drawing a picture, using his daughter as a model. I was considerably amazed to see him try his hand at a portrait, as I had never seen him attempt to paint one before. Most of his paintings were either of extremely simple, fairy-tale type objects or of animals. The picture itself was entirely different from his familiar style. It impressed me as being realistic, delicate, and vivacious. The portrait seemed to possess a spirit and soul of its very own. However, my impression of the painting, in which he had so accurately depicted his subject, was not my initial concern. A sense of hatred surged up from the depths of my heart. The thing which bothered me most was the delicate, subtle atmosphere that hung between my husband and his daughter, pervading the whole studio.

This atmosphere was one of warmth, gentleness, and contentment between a father and his beloved daughter. I had no difficulty understanding such an atmosphere, yet something secretive that I could not interpret also hung in the air; a feeling of intrigue that should not enter a father-daughter relationship.

It was apparent that they wanted to be alone. Although they greeted me politely when I walked into the studio, I felt isolated, as if I were being excluded from their lives.

His daughter's baby, born after three years of marriage, had just celebrated his first birthday. Unlike her appearance when she was single, his daughter seemed illuminated by a dignified splendor, a different phase of beauty. She was lounging on the sofa with perfect poise. Unwillingly, I admired her now at the peak of her youthful beauty.

As I was secretly praising her beauty, a fact flashed through my mind as clear as a bright light. "That's right!" I thought. "His daughter is the same age now as *she* must have been when all that happened." I was comparing his daughter, of course, with his first wife.

During the Korean War, my husband was, of necessity, separated from his first wife. At that time, his wife must have been as young as his daughter is now. This realization shocked me.

His daughter, you see, is not mine; her mother was his first wife. A daughter usually takes after her mother, and my husband's daughter is indeed the exact image of his first wife. My husband must be trying to refresh his memory of his first wife, who was left behind in North Korea.

I am a lot younger than his first wife would be now, but while I am getting older along with my husband, his first wife remains in his heart as a young and beautiful woman just like his daughter. As I was brooding over this, jealousy lifted its head like a poisonous snake. It would be a lot easier for a jealous woman to express her feelings if she had someone's hair to pull, but whose hair could I pull?

Despite my strong feelings, I tried to act normally. Such pretense was indeed agonizing. This sensation of jealousy that couldn't be expressed in any way slowly transformed me into despondency and emptiness, as if I were leading a totally meaningless and worthless life.

I have tried my utmost to live a full life. My husband escaped to South Korea with only his young daughter, leaving his aged parents and his wife behind in the North. When he came to the South, he was penniless and twelve years older than I. He was an unknown artist. At first, I felt sorry for him. My pity for him turned into love, and I eventually married him.

Since then, I have tried to provide love for him and his motherless young daughter. I thought I had succeeded in erasing any insecurity they might feel. I have been loyal to them. Now, I felt victimized as though betrayed by my own efforts to serve them by giving them security and love.

I felt as if I had been cheated. The more I brooded on it, the more troubled I became. I frowned with deep inner conflict. Taking notice of my ugly expression, my husband and daughter inquired solicitously of my health. "Something is bothering me," I said, "and I need to get away by myself for a few days."

"Why do you want to go somewhere alone in this cold weather?" my husband asked after overcoming his initial shock. For the past few days, it had been severely cold. Through the window of my husband's studio, I caught sight of the leafless trees, as bare as skeletons. A nearly deserted frozen street also came into view. Moved by this desolate winter scene, I became choked with emotion. The meaning of my suggestion about taking a trip had been mere childish grumbling, but at that moment, I made up my mind to carry out this plan with no further delay.

All this had nothing to do with any desire on my part to travel, nor to be away from my husband. I wanted to be completely free — free from my life! I had believed I could make this life work through strong will, determination and stubbornness. I now wanted to throw away this precious life of mine as I would a worn-out pair of shoes.

My feeling that I had been leading a life utterly without purpose paralleled the dreary, bitter weather outside. I didn't have the slightest notion what made me yearn for the wintry scenery of a distant place. But I began to make a fuss about leaving immediately. I was not at all concerned about my husband's surprise and bewilderment, nor that of his daughter. In their utopian relationship, they would, I felt, be unaware of my absence.

"My! I have never seen you so hysterical before, my dear," my husband said. Impressed by the fuss I was making, he became quite understanding. He gave me a generous sum of spending money for my trip. He even suggested that it would be good for me to go to a hot-spring resort area since it was wintertime.

When one happens to find out that a treasure previously deemed to be precious is actually fake, one's disgust is bound to be measured by how dearly that treasure was cherished. Immediately casting away such a false treasure could make one happy for the time being. In this mental state, I left my husband to take my trip. I chose the town of On-yang because transportation there was convenient.

Loneliness as well as the wintry chill stalked me on the strange street where I got off the express bus. The town appeared frightfully alien to me. I quite suddenly lost my longing for absolute freedom, and I seriously doubted that I could get used to it.

I was not a unified person. I had only left the city physically; mentally I was still clinging to the old, familiar patterns which had long been a part of me. I couldn't help smiling at this realization.

I headed for a resort hotel but then changed my mind, although I had ample money with me. I checked into an old, modest, second-class hotel instead. It was a chronic habit of mine to question whether or not any item I purchased was genuine, even if I were only buying sesame seed oil. With the same suspicious attitude, I now toyed with doubt about the authenticity of the hot-spring water. Intent upon receiving my money's worth from the hotel, especially for the bath fee, I took repeated baths in spite of my fatigue.

Breakfast was brought to my room the next morning; there were nearly fifteen different side dishes. Although this was only the second meal the hotel had provided for me, I suddenly felt that such food was upsetting my stomach. The meal seemed as dull as if I had partaken of such variety every day. My eyes dimmed with tears because I realized that although it seemed that I had been gone for days, only one day had passed since I left home.

The bellboy asked me if I planned to leave today or if I was going to stay another night. I told him I'd leave early today, fearing that he might feel sorry for me if I replied otherwise. After packing the tiny over-night bag, I went out onto the street. I felt as if I'd been thrown out of the hotel onto the street by the bellboy, and worse, out of my own house by my husband and his daughter.

The intensity of the piercing cold in this town was as severe as that of Seoul. The sky was overcast, and the dark clouds hung low. The mood of the sky, from which swept a biting wind, mirrored the sentiment I had been nurturing — I had, beyond a shadow of a doubt, been leading a purposeless life. The weather reminded me of my life, matching its bitter emptiness.

The street where the resort hotel was located could have fit into the palm of my hand. If I walked around the entire area ten times, it would take less than an hour. I went into the coffee shop in the resort hotel and had a cup of coffee. I did it intentionally in order to be able to give my husband the impression that I had indeed registered at the resort there. To do this, I needed a basic knowledge of the hotel's interior layout.

Across the street from the hotel was the bus station. The old buses with their engines wheezing as if in a state of exhaustion, were stopping for riders. The windshields of the buses were posted with signs stating their destinations, which were unfamiliar to me.

Somehow I felt better, as if my windpipe had just been cleared. Out on the street again, I stopped a passerby and asked where I could find the nearest place of natural beauty and historic interest. The ticket girl on the bus must have overheard my inquiry. She jumped down from the bus that was about to leave, and before I could utter a word, she pushed me onto it like I was some kind of important package. I stumbled before I reached a seat.

The bus was nearly vacant, carrying only a handful of passengers. The vinyl seat was as cold as ice.

"Where is this bus heading?" I asked, seized with uneasiness as the bus quickened speed.

"I'll be sure to let you out by the lake, ma'am," the bus girl said with confidence, as if I had asked her to take me to the lakefront.

"Lake?" I asked.

"Yes, the lake!" she repeated. "It is the only nearby place that's worth seeing. When it is not winter season, ma'am, many people visit the lake, you know."

I hadn't been on the bus two minutes when the girl asked me for bus fare and then nearly pushed me out the door, indicating that we were at the lake.

As she said, there was indeed a lake in front of me, frozen solid and surrounded on all sides by low, bare mountains. It looked murky, gloomy, and opaque, as if the grey sky extended into it. A sudden, gusty whirlwind licked across the surface of the frozen lake and then whipped my cheeks like a cruel lash.

Intimidated, I was about to get back on the bus, but it had already left for the next stop, leaving only swirling dust behind. I wanted to cry from frustration. I hurried to the commercial area by the lake to avoid the biting wind.

At any other time except winter, the place must enjoy a lot of business, for quite a few large signs were still hanging high over the arched gate near the entrance to the area. The signs bore the names of individual businesses in competition with one another for patrons. Now, however, all the restaurants, tea rooms, general stores, and gift shops had their shutters tightly closed.

Not one soul was in sight. The discolored, weather-beaten signs clanked sadly, lashed by the north wind. An air of dreariness permeated the entire place. The ping-pong table by the roadside was nearly buried under snow that must have fallen some time ago. Dust covered the unmelted snow, reminding me of a soiled white sheet. It was a distressing sight.

There was so sign of anyone's presence. I was so lonely that I wished this was all merely a dream. After I walked around the entire commercial section and came out of the area, the frozen lake once again unfolded before me. No one could put a boat into this hard, frozen lake, I thought; furthermore, no one could jump into this lake to drown. The idea did not relieve my distress; instead, it frightened me.

In haste, I looked in a different direction and then began walking along briskly. There was still no sign of people. At the end of the block, however, I saw that the front gate of one house was ajar. The gates appeared to be well kept. A sign reading "Inn" was posted by it. Briquet ashes were piled high between the front and middle gates. I also saw laundry hanging on the clothesline in the inner courtyard. The twisted, frozen white clothes on the line appeared grotesque. I called for the owner of the house in a quivering voice.

A woman in her fifties appeared out of the main house, showing great pleasure at seeing me. When I saw her friendly face, I felt the same sense of relief as I would returning to my own home. I even felt that I'd like her to take care of me. There was some rare quality about her — like a gentle, good, warm, quilted-cotton garment which could shield a person — that was very appealing to me. I felt as if I were recalling a sweet memory of something I had long-since forgotten.

"Do you have a heated room where I can warm myself before I leave?" I asked.

Immediately, the woman, who introduced herself as Mrs. Kim, went ahead to one of the guest rooms in the front wing of the house. She felt the temperature of the floor under the quilt. Then she informed me that the floor was warm enough, but she expressed her concern that the strong wind outside was too severe and would cut through the thin walls. She looked so at a loss that I was concerned about her helplessness and felt sympathetic. I tried to smile as I asked her, "Do I look cold?", but I failed to smile properly because my cheeks were frozen.

"Yes, you look as cold as an icicle. Well, let's go into my own room. The floor is very warm there and I have a stove, too."

After Mrs. Kim extended this invitation, she took my hand and led me freely into her room, as though I were her own sister. The room was as dark as a cave, yet cozy. The curtains were all drawn even though the stove was set to warm the room.

At first I thought no one was in the room. After my eyes became accustomed to the darkness, though, I saw an old woman sitting up straight on the floor. She looked as bony as a dressed-up skeleton. She gave me a blank look, and shook her head back and forth. Her behavior made me think she rejected my presence. For a moment, I stood not knowing what to do with myself. Without realizing how awkward I felt, Mrs. Kim eagerly pulled me down and sat me near the old woman. She had me warm my hands under the quilt on which the old woman was sitting. I saw the old woman's mouth slightly cracking with a smile. She kept on shaking her head, however. Mrs. Kim introduced us. "This is my mother-in-law. Mother, this is a guest. She was so cold that I asked her to come into our room." Thus she explained my presence to her mother-in-law, but she did not explain to me about her mother-in-law shaking her head.

The old woman was thin. Her white hair was neatly combed and put up in a bun. She was dressed in a traditional Korean blouse, which had a clean white collar. She wore a soft wool vest over the blouse. The unique gracefulness in her posture impressed me; such an air of elegance in a place such as this seemed extremely strange to me.

The old woman had begun shaking her head considerably slower. It now seemed to be swaying as a gentle breeze. I hoped she would soon stop shaking her head altogether; my hope, however, proved fruitless.

As my body was warmed, I was overcome by a drowsiness as sweet as honey. The urgent need for a nap became overpowering. I had to sleep even if it killed me.

"Now that I'm warmed up well enough, I'd like to take a nap in the room you showed me earlier. By the way, how often does the bus go to the hot-spring?" I asked.

"During the winter season, only twice a day — once in the morning and once in the afternoon," Mrs. Kim replied. "The bus you came on was the morning route. At about four-thirty in the afternoon the bus will go back to the hot-spring resort area. But what shall I do about your lunch? I'll prepare some food for you. I'd like you to eat before you leave."

My mind became preoccupied with the intensity of my drowsiness. Although I had no appetite for lunch, I told Mrs. Kim to do as she wished. She repeatedly thanked me, bowing her head over and over again. I felt sorry for her, bowing obsequiously again and again just because I had consented to eat lunch. I wondered what sort of profit she could gain from preparing lunch for me.

After I went into the guest room, I sank into a heavy sleep, buried under a thin blanket on the warm, bare floor. Strangely, the thought of the old woman who kept shaking her head popped into my mind as soon as I woke up. As I thought of her, I was uncertain whether I had dreamed about her or had really seen her. Although I was in a hazy state of mind, the image of her shaking her head came into my thoughts distinctly. The curiosity that had been pushed aside by my drowsiness began to nag at me. I looked at my watch; it wasn't even two o'clock yet.

"Are you still sleeping, honored guest? I imagine you're hungry now."

I heard Mrs. Kim's low voice at the sliding lattice-door and arose to open it. Mrs. Kim, wearing her apron, greeted me as I awakened from my nap with the same friendliness that she had shown when I entered her house earlier that day. The warmth of her greeting made me somewhat suspicious. Had she feared that I, her customer, had taken sleeping pills and gone into an eternal sleep?

Before long, Mrs. Kim brought me lunch. It consisted of sesame leaves pickled in soy sauce, fresh green peppers, a wild plant called "tutuk," cabbage and white radish pickles heavily spiced with pepper and garlic, and turnip soup. All these tastefully prepared dishes did not give me the impression of inn food at all. Instead, I felt I as if I were being treated to a home-cooked meal by a relative in the countryside.

Although I was pleased to see such food, my mouth was dry and I had no appetite whatsoever. Seeing that I merely sipped the soup, Mrs. Kim brought me another warm bowl of it. I suggested that she have lunch with me and invited her to sit beside me.

"Thank you kindly, ma'am, but I have already had lunch with my mother-in-law."

Since Mrs. Kim brought up the subject of the old woman, it seemed natural for me to ask about her mother-in-law's strange habit of shaking her head.

"She must have been quite displeased with me," I said. "She didn't say a word, mind you, but she shook her head the whole time I was in your room."

"She has been that way for twenty-five years now."

"For twenty-five years!" I was so amazed that my mouth dropped open.

"Yes, for twenty-five years she has been this way every day, all day long except while asleep."

I could see Mrs. Kim's eyes were getting misty; yet, she spoke in a poised and gentle voice.

Every day for twenty-five years, her mother-in-law has been constantly shaking her head. She ceased to twitch her head only when she was asleep. When she was in good health or a good mood, she shook her head very slightly as if it were being moved by a gentle breeze. When she was feeling poorly, the shaking became more intense and severe. When she was uneasy or there was trouble in the family, she shook her head rigidly and firmly, as if she were desperately trying to say, "I don't know. I don't know. I really don't know."

Hoping to cure her mother-in-law's ailment, Mrs. Kim had used all kinds of Chinese medicinal herbs as well as all the reputable acupuncture treatments within her financial means. In spite of all her efforts, nothing seemed to help her mother-in-law. Mrs. Kim was the first to become discouraged as she and her son tried various treatments. Her dignified mother-in-law, on the other hand, accepted her head shaking as if it were her inevitable fate from which she would be set free only by death.

Her mother-in-law's condition began during the Korean War. Mrs. Kim's young husband had been the chief magistrate of a township. When the war broke out, he could not flee and, as a result, he had to go into hiding. At first he hid in his own house.

The spirit of the new group that took power was extraordinarily bloodthirsty. This development made her exceedingly uneasy and hiding Mrs. Kim's husband in the house became decidedly unsafe.

One night, taking advantage of the dark, Mrs. Kim succeeded in spiriting her husband away to her parents' house located in a valley nestled under the ridge of Gwan-duk Mountain. This task had been arranged secretly between Mrs. Kim and her mother-in-law.

For some unknown reason, the world seemed to be growing worse and worse each day. Calling each other anti-reactionary was a common practice among neighbors and even among relatives. Furthermore, people did not hesitate to denounce one another to the authorities as being anti-reactionary. Not a single day went by without a bloody incident in one of the surrounding villages. Those were terrible times.

As the situation worsened, Mrs. Kim could not rest peacefully. She could not even trust her mother-in-law, who was less aware of current affairs, rigidly honest, and did not know how to be suspicious of others. Considering her mother-in-law's character, Mrs. Kim began to worry about the old woman. Possibly tricked by a neighbor, she might innocently confess her son's whereabouts. The world at that particular time was not a place for people like her mother-in-law.

As if coaching an incompetent student on the multiplication tables, Mrs. Kim taught her mother-in-law the phrase, "I don't know," every day.

"The only thing you need to remember, Mother, is to say that you 'don't know.' Even if an innocent-looking person asks you the whereabouts or your son, you simply say that you don't know anything at all. You tell him your son left the house on the same day that the war broke out, and since that time no one knows what happened to him. You have to put on an innocent air, Mother, and deny any knowledge of his whereabouts. We live in a world where a person's life can be put in danger by someone's careless talk. It takes only one mistake, you know."

"Even if your oldest or youngest son's family inquires," Mrs. Kim had continued, "tell them you have no idea. When the grandmother of this household or that household asks, reply in the same manner as I have instructed you to do, Mother. Please do not trust anyone. Do you understand all this, Mother? Do you?"

Mrs. Kim repeatedly coached her mother-in-law with this "I don't know" phrase, even teaching her to shake her head forcefully. Her mother-in-law always wore a frightened and lost expression on her face, and practiced diligently, saying "I don't know, I really don't know," even when she was alone, shaking her head firmly.

Though it was not a battlefield and not a single enemy gun had been fired, there were still killings in the village. The villagers, who behaved as if they were possessed by evil spirits, killed one another.

Then airplanes suddenly invaded the sky above the quiet village, ceaselessly dropping bombs and strafing with machine guns. For a few days, the sound of gunfire penetrated the village from the surrounding mountains; it sounded as if someone were roasting dried beans in a hot skillet. Following this breakout, a deadly silence fell on the entire village.

The village people, who had been confined inside their houses like trapped mice, appeared one by one outside and then quickly disappeared into their houses again. They were aloof and indifferent, with no conversation or inquiries among themselves.

There was no evidence as to whether the Communist forces had retreated or still surrounded the village. None of the group of pro-Communists, who had once wielded power, was to be seen anymore. However the People's Commission flag, used by the Communists, was still flying in the front courtyard of the house of the person who had been serving as head of the village during this period of war.

During this uncertain, unstable period of time, Mrs. Kim's impatient husband returned home during the late evening hours. His opinion was that the detestable Communists would not be able to sustain their position in the village for even a few days, no matter how desperately they tried. After all, the capital city, Seoul, had already been recovered.

The cabbage seed for the whole winter season had already been planted in the field adjoining the house. A cool wind which would help mature the young, healthy squash on the twig fences was sweeping the air. Making her way through the dew one early morning, Mrs.Kim's mother-in-law went into the back yard to pick some young squash. Suddenly, the silence was broken by a piercing shriek.

"I don't know, I don't know. I really don't know!" she was crying.

At the sound of her mother-in-law's hair raising cry, Mrs. Kim rushed outside, and her husband did the same, before he had time to realize what he was doing. At the time, no one seemed able to stop and think rationally.

At the corner of the outhouse, three or four exhausted shabby People's Republic Army soldiers, who appeared to be stragglers, were all aiming their guns at her mother-in-law. They also looked shocked to find her there. They gave the impression that they had not come there to harm anyone but rather to look for clothing or food. It seemed probable that they were deserters from the Communist Army and had come across her mother-in-law by accident.

Her mother-in-law was still repeatedly crying out, "I don't

know, I don't know," in a strange, high-pitched voice. She was standing motionless, as if her feet were nailed to the ground, and she kept shaking her head as wildly as a mad person. One of the stragglers flashed a murderous look at all of them, fired his gun at random, hitting Mrs. Kim's husband, who dropped heavily to the ground. It was a terrible sight. As the villagers gathered around the fallen man, the soldiers ran away. The whole incident had taken place in a flash.

After that tragic incident, only Mrs. Kim's tireless, faithful devotion in taking care of her nearly insane mother-in-law made recovery possible. Since that fatal day, when she had so violently exerted herself by shaking her head at the straggling soldiers by the corner of the outhouse, her condition had improved. However, the head-shaking had become a chronic habit for the old woman, earning her the nickname of "old woman with a shaking head" throughout the village.

Mrs. Kim told the story in a poised, quiet manner. Although the story had taken some time to tell, she did not seem to ramble in the least.

"The only thing I have in mind now is to try to help her by myself rather than seek medical help," Mrs. Kim stated.

"Help her? What do you mean by that?"

"I realize that she can't help herself, and the head-shaking must be strenuous for her. I've dedicated myself to serving her. I prepare her favorite foods three times a day. I take care of her physical needs, making her as comfortable as I can. I will help her in her great effort until she departs from this world. I'm confident I'll be able to perform this duty for her."

Mrs. Kim referred to her mother-in-law's head-shaking as a "great effort." I wanted to laugh at that but changed my mind and kept my silence. Mrs. Kim's attitude was very serious, making it evident that she was not joking at all. In fact, her face was even mildly radiant with pleasure. She obviously derived a great sense of pride from dutifully performing this task with zeal and fervor.

I could not help but wonder whether or not Mrs. Kim herself was the one carrying out the "great effort," and this thought sent a shiver up my spine.

Mrs. Kim charged me a total of eight hundred won for room and food. I handed her a thousand won and told her to keep the change. She thanked me, bowing her head over and over again. Her flattering behavior made me uncomfortable. Again I wondered what profit she was going to make from serving me lunch, and I wondered once again what made her act so deferentially. After all, I paid only a thousand won for everything.

Mrs. Kim's subservient behavior was not at all becoming to her. In fact, it made her seem awkward, even ridiculous. However, I liked Mrs. Kim very much, even more than I had originally thought I would.

Mrs. Kim put the money carefully into the pocket of her sweater. She looked quite relieved and grateful.

"I'm going to Seoul today with this money, and I'll use it for bus fare." She had once again made a strange statement.

"To Seoul? Why? Why in this cold weather?"

As I uttered "in this cold weather" to Mrs. Kim, I realized I was repeating the exact words that had been said to me by my surprised husband when he had learned of my plans for a trip. Suddenly, I missed him so much that my heart ached.

"My son, my only son, attends a university in Seoul. The baby boy on my back, who watched uncomprehendingly as his father was gunned down so cruelly, has grown up so much. He has already served in the Army, and he is in his junior year now. He is such a nice and reliable boy."

"Oh, I see. By the way, aren't all the schools in winter break?" I asked.

"Yes, that's so, but my son is tutoring some high school students in order to earn money for his tuition. That's why he cannot come down to see us. Even though I make enough money to pay for his tuition, he insists upon doing his share. Every season, except winter, I have a pretty good business here, especially when holidays fall during the tourist season. Then there aren't enough rooms to accommodate all the tourists. Winter is the only time it's so desolate."

"I have carefully put his tuition and money for his room and board for next semester in a safe place," she went on. "I also have stored enough rice and ingredients for all kinds of side dishes to last till the end of winter here. After making their profit, other business people usually close their doors and take it easy at home during this time of year, but I keep this inn open year-round. Because of that, I make it a point to have at least two rooms heated and waiting for prospective customers. My reasons for this are not only for business. Occasionally, people like yourself stop by, not realizing how deserted it is at this time of year. I take great pleasure in providing a customer a warm room when he needs one. That's the truth! The thought of making money is the farthest thing from my mind at moments like that. It would only make me happy if I could buy some meat for my mother-in-law with money from a customer."

She took a deep breath, then began the strange explanation of why I had been so warmly welcomed. "But today is different. Since early morning, I have been waiting for a customer, even carefully calculating the money I was going to make today. Truly, truly ma'am, I have no idea what I would have done if you hadn't dropped in today. Thank you very much, ma'am."

This time Mrs. Kim held my hand tightly instead of bowing. This made me feel a lot better than watching her bow repeatedly. However, I was still puzzled by her demeanor.

"Yesterday, I received an unusual letter from Seoul."

"From your son?"

"No. From the owner of his boarding house. She said in her letter that she hasn't seen my son at her house in over a week now. She wrote further that if my son were an unstable person, she would have felt no need to be fretful or let me know what was going on, but my son has proved to be exceptionally stable and trustworthy in his daily conduct. The woman asked me to come up to Seoul and start an inquiry concerning him. She said she was sticking her neck out just in case something might have happened to him."

"Anyone, even my son, may occasionally act frivolously." She looked intently at me, as if asking me to concur. "I'm sure he is just spending a few nights at a friend's. After all, he doesn't live at home. Do you find it unusual for a person to sleep out when he is boarding some place other than his own home?"

Without waiting for an answer, she posed another question. "What do you think about this woman who upset me so, by sending a letter about such an insignificant matter? Not only do I blame her, but I also blame myself for being too concerned. After receiving such news, you see, my mind became crowded with all kinds of unnecessary, silly notions. I couldn't sleep at all last night. I tossed and turned. Then the wings of my imagination soared, and I managed to invent a superstition to cancel the concern over my son. The superstition goes like this. . ."

"What do you mean you 'invented a superstition'?" I interrupted.

"Yes, ma'am, I know what you're thinking. I'm being preposterous. Anyway, it goes something like this: if I went to Seoul today, with money earned from a customer who needed a room in my inn, no harm would befall my son. On the contrary, if I used part of the money that I have been diligently saving, misfortune would befall my son. Once I settled upon this belief, I had to wait for a prospective customer in anguish and anxiety. Fortunately, you turned out to be the manifestation and the good omen required in my invented superstition. I am so grateful to you, ma'am."

Mrs. Kim thanked me once again. My heart weighed heavily with pity for this widowed woman who tried, by this strange superstition, to mask how troubled she was about the welfare of her only son. I wasn't at all offended by her revelation that she considered me a good sign.

"Then you must be leaving very soon," I commented.

"Yes, indeed. Everything has been taken care of. I have already arranged to have my neighbor attend to my mother-in-law. The only thing left for me to do is wait for the bus. It's scheduled to leave for the hot-spring resort area around four-thirty this afternoon. That will be very soon."

"That means we will be riding the same bus."

"Oh, yes, you're right. You mentioned earlier that you'd ride back to the resort area on the four-thirty bus."

"Well, I'll be going all the way to Seoul with you," I said.

At the spur of the moment, I had decided to return to Seoul that day. Once I made up my mind, I felt a surge of relief.

When Mrs. Kim went into her room to bid farewell to her mother-in-law, I accompanied her. The two of them clasped each other's aged, weather-beaten hands tightly. I couldn't tell which belonged to whom.

"Mother, I need to go to Seoul today. I have a few things to buy, and I would also like to see Tae-sik, who couldn't come to see us during the winter break as he had to study. I miss him so. The girl from next door, Sam-soon, will take good care of you, Mother, while I'm gone. Don't worry about anything, and try to eat a lot at every meal."

Whether the old woman understood her daughter-in-law or not, she still continued to shake her head ever so gently. Her head-shaking impressed me, as if she were saying, "My dear daughter, your son Tae-sik is all right. Please believe me, he is just fine, I tell you. We haven't done anything sinful to hurt anyone. Why should you fret that some misfortune has come to him?"

Abruptly, I had the urge to put my hand over their tightly clasped hands. The friendly hands of two strangers, the hands of partners who had been carrying out a great effort together. There was something that flowed strongly through the veins of their hands. I wanted to feel this pulse myself. I wanted to touch their hands with my own and then cherish that special feeling in my heart for a long time.

As if it were the first and last chance for me to touch the one thing left in the world which was not empty, not void, I put my hand over theirs as my heart desired. I did it gratefully and humbly. My weak, pale hand covered their two warm, rough ones.

"Take care of yourself, ma'am," I said.

Even though the old woman shook her head gently at my farewell, I had a feeling that she was saying, "Your life hasn't been as meaningless as you think. You haven't lived that way at all, my dear! No, you haven't indeed!"

Translated by Hyun-jae Yee Sallee

Notes on the Authors

Chung-joon Yee is the author of the title story, *The Snowy Road.* Yee's works are given a distinctive character by his talent for plumbing the greatest depths to uncover the true meaning of an incident and thus hold more meaning for a reader willing to read between the lines. Yee received one of Korea's most prestigious literary awards, the Lee Sang Award, in 1978. One of his major works is a collection of short stories, *Winter Square,* which enjoyed a record thirteen printings in Korea.

Yean-hee Chung, author of *Balloon,* is critically acclaimed in Korea as an important and influential contemporary writer. She has received numerous literary awards, including the Korean Literature Writers Award. She has travelled extensively to many parts of the world and is currently a part-time instructor at Ewha Women's University in Seoul. Her favorite themes are showing the inner strength and virtue of endurance displayed by ordinary people facing life's daily challenges.

Wan-suh Park, author of *Winter Outing*, is the most prolific and one of the best-known women authors writing in Korea today. She started her writing career in her early forties and has vigorously demonstrated her story-telling talent and her keen perception of life. She tells a story with a candid outlook combined with compassion. Combining a candid outlook with compassion, her unique style brings the reader a sense of hope despite the pathos and despair in life.

Bum-shin Park, author of *The Trap*, is best known for his novel *Fire Country*. Mr. Park is a respected and beloved author in Korea and an active member of PEN. The war-torn Korea of nearly four decades ago and its aftermath as reflected in family and society are favored themes in his work. He is the recipient of a literary award sponsored by the Korean Culture and Arts Foundation. A part-time university instructor, he devotes his life to creative writing.

Ick-suh Yoo, author of *Purchased Bridegroom*, achieved fame with his novel *Abel's Hours*. His work centers on the innermost feelings of the less fortunate man. His protagonists are victims of rapidly changing economic and social conditions in modern Korea. His pen is as sharp as a knife; he penetrates into the mind of the reader to ask, "Can your conscience be clear when you continue to overlook such injustice in our society?" For the past few years, Mr. Yoo has been interested in folk music, and he has begun to use folklore as the basis for his plots.

Jung-rae Cho is the author of *Echo, Echo*. Mr. Cho's work concentrates on the era of turmoil when Korea was under Japanese rule and on the political, economic, and social chaos of the early sixties. He brings a balanced perspective to daily problems, and although his characters are directionless at times, they transcend human suffering and hardship with much courage.

Notes on the Translators

Hyun-jae Yee Sallee, a native Korean, has been translating Korean literature for over six years. Her first translated novel, *The Waves*, published in 1989 by Kegan Paul International, London, England, was critically acclaimed. Her short story translations have most recently appeared in an anthology of Korean fiction published in Australia in 1990. She was the recipient of a translation award sponsored by the Korean Culture and Arts Foundation in 1989. Ms. Sallee is a full-time employee at Walt Disney World in Orlando, Florida. She currently lives in Kissimmee with her husband, Rawleigh, and their two children, Sarah and Ike.

Dr. Teresa Margadonna Hyun, a professor of French and Comparative Literature at Kyung Hee University, Seoul, Korea, has published extensively on East-West literary and cultural relations and her articles on translation theory have appeared in various journals. She is currently completing study on translation, culture, and the reshaping of traditions during the formative phase of modern Korean literature.